88 ~~Eight~~ Guys for Coffee

by
Diane Solomon

88 Guys for Coffee
by Diane Solomon

Eloquent Rascals Publishing
Hillsborough, NH

Website:
http://www.EloquentRascals.com

All rights reserved. No part of this book may be reproduced or transmitted in any form or by any means, electronic or mechanical, including photocopying, recording, or by any information storage and retrieval system, without written permission from the author, except for the inclusion of brief quotations in a review.

Copyright ©2017 by Diane Solomon
First Edition
ISBN: 978-0-9907094-8-0

Dedication

    This book is dedicated to Valerie, my dearest sister-friend. You are family. You were there for me during the rough, and you celebrate with me during the golden.

    And, to my husband, Mark. After a very long search, I found you. These luscious years with you have been bliss.

Introduction

As I began my dating quest/mission/slog, I discovered that many of my experiences belonged in the realm of the bizarre or hilarious. I entertained a few of my friends with these stories and more than one exclaimed, "You simply must write a book!" I demurred, feeling that there must be enough books about online dating by this time. My friend David's response was, "Is there only one cookbook?" I see his point.

This book is a "Fictional Memoir," a genre I did not know existed until I hunted around to decide what genre my book was going to fit in! This means the book is part truth, and part fiction. The stories about dating are absolutely true, as word for word as I could get them. Except, of course, I changed names, appearance, locations, and careers of the guys I met. This to save embarrassment and maybe a potential libel lawsuit... Ahem.

Laura, the main character, is mostly from my imagination. Her personal story, personality, her career path, her feelings and thoughts are all fiction. She is a composite of various people I have known, with a little of me thrown in. I decided not to write the book from my own perspective, as that would have been a bit too painful. Also, Laura is an interesting soul, and I think, a better person than I am. It was fun to live in her heart and mind during the writing! I *know* me, so that might have been boring. For you, perhaps. To me, certainly.

There are invaluable tips to the online dating newbie in this tale, as well as some laughs. Also, I hope to provoke some thought into the crazy world of man-woman relationships, and, indeed, how to be a human being this lifetime. I think there should be courses on how to be human, as sometimes I do think we have lost track.

Enjoy!

Warmly,

Diane Solomon,
Spring 2017

Acknowledgements

Jim Herity, author of **_On Anvil_**. Jim contributed quite a few of "Hank's" lines and thoughts in this book. These are real! That's how smart and funny Jim Herity is. Check out his wonderful first novel, _On Anvil_. I hope there are many more books to come.

Editor: T. B. Wolff

Beta readers and/or from all over the country: Valerie Torphy, Cindy Jevarjian, Cheryl Kareff, Jan James, Laurie Seymour, Laura Carey, Marsha Campaniello, Deb Whitman, Cheryl Karney, Thelma Tracy. Thank you so much for your input and suggestions!

Prologue

*I was born when you kissed me. I died when you left me.
I lived a few weeks while you loved me.*
~ Humphrey Bogart

"Somewhere after my third marriage, I sobered up... and realized I was gay."

Excuse me?

On an unusually hot, even sweltering day in May, I was propped up against the deli counter of my local Stop and Shop. It felt good to bask in the cool air.

Stifling a grin, I glanced around and identified the source of this exceptional remark. An elderly, artistic-looking gentleman was squeezing a rather firm ball of Mozzarella cheese, sniffing it. He was with a friend, and yes, he too was male. His younger companion smiled at him and gave his older "friend's" arm a little chug. What is a chug? A sort of squeezy, comforting shake... a chug. As I headed home, air conditioner and Keith Urban blasting, I grinned. I was happy for them. Not so happy for the three women who had not been privy to their husband's predilections. Still, I know he meant well.

Tapping the remote on the car visor, I pulled into my garage and hopped out. Grabbing the groceries, I could hear the phone ringing inside the townhouse, but I knew in this heat I couldn't (or just damn well wouldn't) hurtle up the stairs to get it before the machine clicked on. Besides, anyone I wanted to talk to had my cell phone number.

Climbing up the stairs with more bags than I could easily carry (and hoping that bang against the stair rail was not bad news for the eggs), I heard a voice leaving a message. It was a woman, so it wasn't Kurt. Due home from Maryland in a couple of hours, I thought he might be letting me know where he was. He loathed the infamous New Jersey turnpike, but I'd given him the incentive to endure it: his favorite mushroom omelet with feta cheese for lunch.

I carefully put the bags down on the kitchen counter, peeked to see the eggs were still intact, and punched the voice message playback.

"Hi, Mr. Phillips, this is Stacey from Mahoney Movers. I sure hope the move went well for you. Uh, we have a little problem here, though. Could you give me a call as soon as possible, please? The credit card we have had on file for you for your storage costs is now not clearing for the move. It has expired and I need your new info. Please give me a call. Thanks. Bye now."

You know how when you hear something shocking, there can be a sort of time delay, where your brain rushes through all the denial statements, the "there must be some mistake" and the "what the hell is she talking about" responses, while the whole time there is a rush of knowing, of understanding, because you suddenly get it. You *get it*. It all suddenly comes together. How distant he had been on the phone for each of the four days he had been down in Maryland seeing his folks and his grown kids. How he'd stayed two days longer than he originally told you he'd planned to stay. The fact that you'd seen a couple of his emails several months ago from a rental agency about a townhouse near his family in Fulton. But, when you asked him about it, he said he was looking for his son, who was too busy to look for himself. You had bought it. Hook, line, and stinker. Trusted that what he said was the truth. Why wouldn't it be? His son had been looking for a new place.

I grabbed the phone and redialed the last number.

"Stacey, please." This was in my best chirpy fashion, still praying there was some dreadful mistake. As I waited for her to pick up her extension, I felt the cold goose bumps come up on my arms. I don't keep the house that cool; it wasn't the AC. I nearly slammed down the phone, suddenly not wanting to know.

Absolutely... not wanting to know.

"Stacey Mahoney."

"Hi Stacey, Laura Phillips, here, do you remember me? You guys moved Kurt and me to Connecticut last year?"

"Hey, Laura, sure, nice to hear from you, how are you?"

"Great, thanks. I just got your message. Kurt won't be back for a couple of hours, can I help?

She explained the problem, but asked very kindly again whether the move had gone well. I said that it had, and asked if she had the correct address there in front of her, for future correspondence with us.

I couldn't believe how clearly I was thinking, how friendly and efficient I was on the phone with this woman, who was the harbinger of complete disaster, of complete heartbreak. Who was about to give me information that would either settle my heart. Or break it.

I quickly scribbled down the address in Fulton, near Baltimore, that she gave me, and responded. Yes, of course, that was right. I couldn't let her know this was the first time I'd ever heard of it. Couldn't have dealt with questions.

Oh yes, we are settling in fine. What? No, doesn't look like any damage, thanks. Still smiling and operating in autopilot stupor, I managed to tell her I didn't have the updated credit card info on me, but Kurt would call her in a couple of hours.

With a thundering in my ears, I somehow got through the nice parting noises you are supposed to make, and hung up the phone.

Then slithered down to the floor, in a pile, right there on the kitchen floor.

I couldn't breathe.

He'd moved. We'd been married for seven years, and half our stuff had been in storage. We'd moved to Connecticut 18 months ago and had decided to rent while we looked for the right house to buy. But, he'd decided to move back to the Baltimore area, where he grew up, without talking it over with me. He'd looked for a house, signed a lease, and had all our stored furniture moved there. And hid it from me. Only a week ago, we'd driven all over Fairfield County looking at houses for sale. He was looking at houses with me in

Connecticut, while he had already signed a lease on a house for himself in Maryland.

I just sat there. I don't know how long. My handbag had spilled out all over the kitchen floor, and I stared at the little roll of Lifesavers, now lodged under the fridge. All I could get my brain to think was that I must collect those mints. They were Lifesavers, after all. Appropriate. The only other thing that registered was that the porcelain tile beneath my bare legs felt nice and cool. So nice and cool.

I sat there. Time didn't hold any meaning. Suddenly, something cold and wet hit my shoulder, and I jumped. I looked up to see that the frozen yogurt from a shopping bag had rolled out, fallen on its side, and the lid had come off. Now it was melting away sadly and dripping down on me. Organic vanilla frozen yogurt. Blop. Blop.

I heaved myself off the floor, suddenly an aged person, and stumbled into the living room, one leg completely asleep. Feeling as if I were peering at my surroundings through the wrong end of a telescope, I felt removed from everything, nothing looked right. I shivered and sank into the couch at the far end of the room and waited. I didn't think. I just waited.

The front door jiggled, keys turned, the door burst open, and I heard his voice.

"Hey, I'm home!"

"Hello..." I called out weakly, my heart pounding so hard I thought he'd hear it over my greeting.

"Hey, where are you?" He headed towards me, but stopped short. He must have seen my face.

Much later, when I looked in a mirror, I saw the different woman I had become in that horrid couple of hours. Haggard, face streaked with tears and eye makeup, pale, eyes wide and shocked. A different face.

"Oh my God, are you OK?" He hurried towards me. I held up my hand to stop him, to keep him at a distance. I couldn't bear for him to get near me.

"The movers called, Kurt. They need your new credit card info."

He stared at me. There was a long, sickening silence. I felt as though I were viewing this sorry situation from outside of my own body. My spirit remained detached, protecting itself, disassociated from the pain of the woman in denial on that couch.

"Tell me the truth, Kurt, for God's sake. Just tell me the truth." I was cold. And still.

"How much do you know?"

This was his response?

"How much do I know? Seriously, Kurt, how much do I *know*?"

The moment snapped. I was thrust painfully and furiously to life. I dragged it out of him.

I'm not going to share all the gory details. He had moved out, in effect he had left me. Just like that. He was just back to try to figure out how to tell me. I cried, I wailed, and I screamed. The next three hours were full of "how dare you," "how could you," and "but we looked at all those houses last weekend…"

He said, at one point in this hell, "I'm so sorry, Laura, but I stayed two years longer than I wanted to..."

"Big of you. Get out."

He did.

I had to climb straight back into my car and drive to Massachusetts to take my mom to get her passport renewed, for her upcoming trip to see her sister in England. Because when the sky has fallen, your house burns down, or your heart is broken, you still have to go pick up your 76-year-old mother and take her to Boston to get her passport renewed.

Like nothing on earth had happened.

Chapter 1

Back In the Saddle Again ♪

or

The Man with the Minus Touch

*"If you kiss on the first date and it's not right,
then there will be no second date."*
~ Jennifer Lopez

Meeting a guy for coffee. Ok, here I go, I thought. I can do this. Having decided to dip my toe back into the endless pool of available men on online dating sites, I was therefore Back In The Game. Does it have to be a game?

It was warm, still summer-muggy, and good old I-95 was jammed, as usual. I guess you could say it was a parking lot more often than a freeway. Now mid-afternoon, I realized getting back to my place, north of Fairfield, at five or six o'clock would be a pig. The Merritt Parkway would be even worse; Kurt used to say he didn't know what Connecticut had done to God, but the Merritt Parkway was His retribution. I hadn't thought about that when I suggested four o'clock at a coffee place in Stamford. Ah well, too late, now.

I was driving carefully, so as not to mess up my newly painted fingernails. I had taken pains to look great for this first trek out into the world again, and that certainly included drop-dead red fingernails. I'd curled my long dark hair just enough to give it that soft wave that looked natural. Like you woke up like that. Yeah, right. There was no way I'd open the window; even a little breeze would mess with the effort I'd made to look like I'd done nothing.

I was wearing my favorite pair of stretchy jeans with blingy sandals, a red knit tank top that was just snug enough, if you know what I mean. Casual, with just a soupçon of glamour and sexiness. (Bigger than a smidge and smaller than a bucket load. I had to look it up).

You go for it, babe.

It had been a terrible few months. I could relate to that scene in *Something's Gotta Give* where Diane Keaton weeps and wails her heart out over Jack Nicolson. That was me. It just didn't seem as funny as it had in the movie. Not funny at all.

There were times when I just had to creep into the closet, sit under his remaining jackets and shirts, and hide, feeling like a little wounded animal. There were times when I woke in the middle of the night and wondered, for a very brief moment, what the grim feeling circling my solar plexus was. That strange there's-a-vulture-somewhere feeling. Then reality would hit. A physical punch in the stomach that literally knocked the breath out of me and left me doubled over and gasping.

And, the worst moment, I think, was when I had a dream about Kurt, where I was begging him, with all the strength of my being, not to leave me. Things you'd never do in your waking life are acted out in all their ferocious intensity in your dreams. You feel it, smell it, and visualize it in glorious Technicolor, with all sensation turned up to maximum power.

I managed to keep body and soul relatively together during this time. I worked at the clinic – I'm a naturopath – and fed my little velvety black cat, Pusskin. Most days, I even managed to keep one foot plodding in front of the other on my nightly walk/jog around my townhouse complex. I felt hollowed out inside. I was surprised that with the lightest breeze, I didn't just blow away.

It's funny, though, how the habits and routine of existence kick in to make the hours go by, food go down, smiles at strangers happen, just like you were fine, normal, part of the human family. But, I was removed. Part of me had died.

I spent three or four dreadful months crying, writing poetry or song lyrics, and trying to overcome denial, shock, and grief. Then, I hesitantly crept onto Match.com, some weird site called "Plenty of Fish," and a couple of other online dating sites.

My friend, Francesca, had been nudging me for several weeks to "get back on the horse," which felt to me more like an ass, and try it again. She wanted me to "be in the company of a nice man," as she put it. She wanted me to find someone who would be very, very good to me. Yeah, right. The problem with that notion? I couldn't believe there was any male left on earth who would be good to me. I felt that all men were hateful, lying scumbags.

That having been said, there I was on my way to meet someone (poor guy) for a first cup of coffee. Was I ready for this? Well, hell, I figured you have to start somewhere. Some poor man had to be my first foray into the world of being "out there," as it was so succinctly put in *When Harry Met Sally*.

The first man I was meeting was a gem distributor, Jim, was his name. (I kept thinking of him as Jim-Gem, to help me remember his name...). Attractive, if not handsome, we exchanged a couple of emails before he did the gentlemanly thing and gave me a phone number. We had a short chat on the phone, then picked a time to meet, and there I was, headed to meet him in a cute little coffee shop I knew of in Stamford.

I arrived before he did, and found a table next to the window. Checking my hair and lipstick in my compact, then playing with my phone to look busy, I glanced up surreptitiously from time to time to check who was coming through the door. I only waited a minute or two, then saw a man at the door who might be him. He was gazing around, for me, obviously. I raised my hand and he spotted me.

My first impression of Jim-Gem didn't knock my socks off, but something inside told me that after the hurt Kurt had caused, my socks were firmly and permanently glued to my feet.

My date turned out to be an average guy: average looks, average height, average weight, and rather average (read boring) personality. In fact, everything about him was average, except his ego, which was enormous. Especially about his business. The man bought and sold jewels, for crying out loud. Diamonds, rubies, emeralds... What's not to like about that? Bringing your work home, dear? Sure, hang it around my neck! I could feel my socks loosening a tiny bit... until he started to talk. And talk. And talk. Gems, facets, carets, blah blah blah. Zzzzzzz. If I wanted to yawn, I could have stayed home.

He could grind the Crown Jewels into a bag of dust with his voice alone.

I sat there. I realized this was not going to work. There was no "meeting of the minds." No spark. In fact, I feared I was losing consciousness.

Oh, for a roll of duct tape.

Just in time, he altered the course of the conversation. What did he alter it to? A rigorous grilling, by him of me: what did I want, did I have kids, did I like kids, was I happy in this area, would I consider moving (he lived an hour away), was I a morning person? Was I night person? Did I have any moles that might be cancerous?

Did I say it was a conversation? For him, maybe. But, for me it felt a little like an interview. A *lot* like an interview. I guess it was, in some ways. He was looking for someone to fill the position of pandering to his ego.

I should have gone to the ladies room and climbed out the window.

I didn't.

Instead, I hung in there, thinking I must *not* judge so quickly or so harshly, and must give people a chance. After all, I was a sophisticated grown up. I even justified it to myself that it was good to have an airing of desires, wishes, lifestyle comparisons, and such, so as not to waste time.

Nope. Sorry. This Jim could have been Diamond Jim Brady for all I cared. I wanted to go home, gather Pusskin onto my lap, get my feet up in my big leather chair, and stare at the tube.

I stole a glance at my watch. If I could wind this down, see this bozo in my rear view mirror, I could get home in time for *Grey's Anatomy* or curl up with a Nora Roberts novel. If I couldn't find any passion or romance in my own life, I'd damn well get some vicarious thrills there.

Just as I was preparing my leaving excuses, his son joined us, who had just completed some errands in town. Nice enough kid, about 17, who was polite but clearly not interested. He'd seen it all before. Dad doing his thing.

Jim-Gem helped me on with my jacket.

"So, Laura, where did you park, can we drive you to your car?"

"I'm a couple of blocks down, on a meter – that would be great, thanks."

He told me his car was right outside. It was raining lightly, and since I didn't think he and his son were the rapist-team type, I felt OK about accepting the short lift.

He helped me into his brand new, blue, late-model Mercedes sedan. Leather seats and a spacecraft dashboard. And ah, that new car smell. Comes in a can for the rest of us poor shmucks.

"Gorgeous," I said with enthusiasm.

"Just picked it up today," he replied. So proud he was, like a new dad.

He drove me to my little eight-year-old Honda CRV, where his son hopped out, having spied some friends of his on the sidewalk.

As I turned back towards him to say my thanks and good-byes, he suddenly grabbed me, and kissed me. Hard. He pushed his tongue into my mouth, which had only opened in complete shock. I didn't fight back; it all happened too quickly, and afterwards I remembered I didn't want to offend him by pulling away. What? Who the hell was offensive here? After his quick, hard, dipstick "kiss," he pulled back, and nodded briefly. For a second, I thought he was going to offer to check my tires and clean my windshield.

"Good," he said. "That works." Gee, I guess I passed inspection. Oh, yay me.

I politely (yes, I was still polite) said my good-byes, jumped out, hopped in my car and tore away as quickly as possible.

Future messages remained unanswered. I didn't feel I owed him anything at all.

Let him interview and tongue-check some other poor fool.

Gem distributor... oh well.

He turned out to be the man with the minus touch.

Chapter 2

Back in the Cave

*"Think you're escaping and run into yourself.
Longest way round is the shortest way home."*
~ James Joyce

"Ok, that's me done, I'm not ready for this. Cave, here I come. I'm sure glad I didn't give that whack-doodle my phone number."

I asked Siri to phone Francesca, the very minute my car was headed away from the little coffee house. I just needed to talk with a sane person. And Francesca is extremely sane, very wise, and very loving. Lucky me.

Ever positive, she was encouraging.

"Ah, well, honey, there's always an idiot to get through – just bad luck you started with him. At least he was just boring, not scary, somehow... The tongue thing is a bit weird. Ewwww. But never mind. Don't let this discourage you. . Just make a date with someone else. Quickly – don't think about it too much, or else this will freak you out. I know you must have dozens of other men in your inbox."

"Oh, I don't know about that. I'm not feeling very confident... The whole dating thing – it seems so foreign. And I'm 45, now, not the young 29-year-old every guy seems to want to meet."

Her reply was emphatic. "Are you kidding me? Any man who sees your picture will fall all over himself to get to you. You're drop-dead gorgeous. Your problem is going to be beating them off."

"Oh, sweetie, you're so kind... But I really have to double up on the Pilates sessions. Oh, for the days when I was so young and in shape that I couldn't store a pencil under my butt cheek... It would fall right down. Ever tried that?"

"Uh, not lately," said Francesca, through her laughter.

"Well, somewhere around 35 or 40 that damned pencil began to just stay there," I said. "Held by the descending cheek. I don't want to be able to tuck one in there and have it still be there in a decade. Anyway, I guess I'll be content, as long as I don't get so fat that I can store a subway sandwich in there."

I realized I'd been distracted by our chit-chat, and had driven mindlessly off down a road I'd never been on before. I saw a bit late that I was facing away from I-95, and was heading north through the beautiful northern wilds of Stamford. A U-turn was not an easy option on this cramped back road. If I was in my VW beetle from years ago, I could have managed it. That little car turned on a dime. Geez, my CRV won't even turn on a buck and a quarter.

Ah well, I'll take the Merritt Parkway, I like it better anyway. To hell with what Kurt used to say about it…

Kurt... Come on, Laura, don't go there. Stop looking back. Just think of the lovely parkway. Even with rush hour traffic on it, the winding highway through the trees of Connecticut sure beat the truck-laden I-95 any day.

I set the GPS for home. To the cave.

"I just don't think I am ready for dating yet, Francesca."

"You'll never feel ready, you know. So, you may as well just keep going. And I can't stand to see you sit around and pine for Kurt. Damn it, he is not worth another second of your time or heart."

Her outrage brought a tremble to her voice when she mentioned Kurt. When I had told her that he wanted to come up to collect the rest of his stuff, she had seethed with rage.

"If it were me, I'd throw it all out on the front lawn and set fire to it, just in time for him to pull up and see the mighty blaze," she said. "I'll help you."

Francesca is Italian, feisty, not a self-worth issue in sight, and I love her dearly. We had met by accident, one of pure providence, as it happened. She lives near me, and on my walks, I was in awe of her gorgeous garden and conservatory full of plants, and I knew there was the possibility of a kindred spirit.

When we met, over the pruning of roses, I couldn't believe a woman could look that beautiful in old jeans, sweatshirt and pruning gloves. She looked like Natalie Wood; how great would that be? She exists in this life in a perpetual state of glamour, style, and confidence. When I garden, I look like an old farmer.

We had lunch for six hours. We can talk forever and never run out of conversation. Both single, we had a great deal in common: we both loved plants, gardening, theater, and music. Also, neither of us had been fortunate enough to have children, this lifetime. In my case, this may have been just as well, as parenting is not for the meek. Watching my friends and family bring up kids, I wonder how on earth they do it. I admire and respect their courage.

Francesca and I became the kind of deep friends only women can achieve, connecting on so many levels: from Russian Sage in our gardens to the brand of tampons in our bathrooms, from our philosophy of cats to our yearning for God. We supported each other's decisions, no matter what.

We are both passionate, sensitive women, although I envy Francesca's practicality. I need to work on that.

We held onto each other and it helped. It really, really helped.

"Are you coming over tonight?" I asked. "My turn to cook."

"Looking forward to it – see you later, honey."

45 years old and I had to start over. I knew that one third of people over 40 are single, but that certainly didn't make it any easier for me. Just because there were plenty of other people in the same boat, this didn't make me feel any better about it. I get seasick terribly easily, like in a Jacuzzi tub – spare me from any kind of boat!

Being on my own was the last thing in the world I wanted – I didn't choose it. I thought I had found my place at last, thought I'd found home. But, then, we had survived some trouble a couple of years earlier, when, after a nonsense fight of some sort, he had withdrawn his love, his affection, his touch. For months. I was terrified and lonely. But I thought we were past all that – it was at least two years ago! We had just been looking at houses, this past weekend, for goodness sake.

What an adept and callous liar. And a coward. He couldn't bring himself to talk to me about what he'd decided to do. About the unilateral decision, he'd made about *our* lives. No, he just spent six months looking for another place to live, sorted out with his firm to return to the home office, and slithered away without telling me.

I sighed, as I pulled into my garage. My coffee date had certainly been less than stellar. I was glad I had the evening with Francesca to look forward to.

She and I cooked for each other one night a week, so at least we would eat well that one evening. Health nut though I am, (uh, I mean, I am a naturopath, after all), I confess to eating a bowl of breakfast cereal some nights, or just a piece of toast and some yogurt. Or, occasionally I'd just boil up frozen peas. All by themselves. Just a big ole' bowl o' peas. Don't tell anyone – I loved it.

Mild, for an evening in September, we were out on the small wooden deck behind my townhouse. We were sucking up the last of the sensation of warm night air on our bare arms and legs before it became just a memory with the onslaught of the New England winter. Garlic grilled asparagus and roasted herb chicken, one of our standard dinners, was nothing but a spot of grease on each plate, and she reached for her cigarettes. Although I worry about her smoking, I love her enough not to bug her about it. I'd delivered my spiel, once, months ago, and that was it. I would not nag.

"How goes it with Keith?" I asked. Having shared the story of my first dating encounter with Jim-Gem-Man, I'd bored myself all over again just telling the tale. Now, I was more than eager to change the subject.

Francesca was full to bursting about her new man. "It just gets better and better. I lived with William for all those years and loved him with all my heart. Now I just can't believe I could be this lucky to find love twice."

She had married young, to her dear William, and reveled in a wonderful marriage for 25 years. She devotedly cared for him the last three years of his life, as he died from a rare and devastating neurological disease. Now, at 49, she had been alone for a year and a half, and was deep into wondering what the hell the rest of her life was for. What it would bring. What she wanted. She didn't know, and it mortified her. Newly into a relationship with an incredibly interesting, vital, charismatic man, she didn't know where it fit in the scheme of things.

She didn't even have to battle the weird online dating scene. She met him through her work, and they "knew" the moment they laid eyes on each other. It gives me hope, although I only met sick people, as a naturopath, and 80% of them were women, at that. And, since practitioner/patient conversations often involved constipation or acne (throw in a little phlegm), you can see that my work abides in the realm of the Non-Romantic. There's not a lot of room for, "Hey, ya wanna have dinner?"

However, the old-school way of meeting a man had worked out well for Francesca. She had created her own successful home-staging business, and a realtor colleague of hers had referred her to a homeowner who needed her services. The homeowner? It was Keith. A successful attorney in the area, and newly divorced, he was trying to sell his house in the terrible recession following the 2008 mess. He wanted someone to give it every advantage in the marketplace, and knew that a good home-stager does this.

Francesca and Keith took one look at each other and went to have dinner, ostensibly to talk about the way the house could best be presented. But, in actual fact, to learn all they could about each other and fall wildly in love. Amazing. He later told me he watched her walk up the driveway and he was "toast." That's the term he used. Toast! Totally done for. I love that an attorney considering a run for Congress could use the word "toast" where a woman is concerned.

"Is it as good as it was with William?" I enquired.

In the fading light, the tip of her cigarette glowed and crackled as she pulled in on it. I listened to the Peepers hollering away out in the woods, as if their lives depended on it. Maybe they did. Or, maybe they were just happily doing what Peepers do.

"It's different," she said after a few moments thought. "You know, I think every relationship is different because it is a different pairing. Two people bring such unique qualities to a relationship, how could it be the same as any other?"

With that thought, she stubbed out her cigarette in the old planter full of sand she used as an ashtray when she was at my place, and headed off to the powder room.

I slapped a late season mosquito off my leg, and thought about what she said. I knew deep in my bones I could never love again…

But, I guess one of my flaws is that I tend to be an all-or-nothing person, kind of black or white. I keep reminding myself not to be this way, but have you noticed that reminding yourself doesn't change anything much?

I was suddenly a bit chilled, out there on the deck in the night air. I shivered.

Francesca returned at last. She'd been gone awhile and I was starting to wonder, when she appeared, pulling the patio slider door closed behind her. She was carrying a cup of English Breakfast tea for me (oh, bless her, I was just thinking how nice that would be) and the bottle of wine from the kitchen to top off her own glass.

"This wine is lovely. Oh, wait, it's too dark to read the label out here... What is it?" She savored a sip.

"Hmmm. Which one did I open? Was it the Chateau Wednesday?"

She did a mini double take, grinned and held the glass up in a toast to me. Then, she settled back in her chair and gazed away across the grounds, dimly lit now by the solar lamps scattered along the paths and driveways.

We were silent for a few moments, then she glanced at her watch.

"I should go home in a bit. The kitchen is a mess, can I help you clean up?"

"Not in a million years. And ruin this night? It's the vegetable roasting pan, it has to be soaked. What a mess that makes. Maybe we should be like the Russians. They don't eat vegetables... they just soak a cow in vodka."

Francesca chuckled.

She drained her glass and said, "I was thinking... Men just take so damn much looking after. You know, the other night, when Keith was there, he went to the fridge, stood there for five minutes, then called over his shoulder to me in the other room, 'Hey Fran, do we have any half-and-half?' (You know how I hate being called Fran. Why do I let him call me Fran?)" She shrugged. "Anyway," she continued, "I had to get up, come into the kitchen, look around him into the fridge, and there, right in front, was the half-and-half. 'Hey thanks, babe,' was his reply. Embarrassed he hadn't seen it? Apologetic I had gotten up and left what I was doing? Nah." She shook her head.

I chuckled. I couldn't believe it – I thought I was the only one who had experienced this.

"Oh my God, you too?" I asked. "With Kurt it was the mayonnaise. He'd asked me if there was any mayonnaise. Same story, it was always there, in the fridge, right in the front row. If it'd been a mountain lion, I'd be a widow, instead of a soon-to-be divorcee."

Francesca laughed, then I laughed, then she laughed at my laugh, and then I breathed in wrong and nearly choked. But we couldn't stop. Once you start laughing, even mildly amusing things seem hilarious. Which is the seed from which "You had to be there" stems.

We wiped our eyes and recovered ourselves. The night was just so special, and warm, and I could hear the little stream behind the deck burbling away, merrily. The last of the crickets and those Peepers, again, noisy in the night, were desperately hoping to extend the warm weather, just a little longer. Weren't we all?

Chapter 3

You Can't Make This Stuff Up

*I think once you enter the dating world
and you realize it's nothing like those Disney
movies you watched when you were a little
girl, you just become more guarded.*
~ Megan Fox

OK, let's try this again. I had met two or three more men for a cup of coffee, with varying results. All less than stellar. None culminating in a second date.

These experiences had succeeded in one aspect, however. They had pushed me headlong into Stage Two of online dating.

I'd better explain. Stage One is best expressed as the Romantic Horsemanure stage. At first, I thought there should be a regular slew of e-mails back and forth and maybe a few phone calls. Wooing... I lived with the flaky, floaty notion that being pen pals and connecting a bit on the soul level before you actually met was a wonderful idea. Jane Austen-esque letters. Ha! What a complete frickin' waste of life.

Stage Two is when Stage One is just not panning out. You have been talking for a month and nothing at all is happening. So you completely flip your methodology. You decide that the best way to move things along is just to make sure the guy doesn't have a voice like a chipmunk, isn't a complete narcissist or a chain-saw murderer, and has some sense of humor. Then you just get on with it. Meet him and have a cup of coffee, for goodness sake.

This is what I did. Because, otherwise I'd found I could invest many hours and tons of brain lobes trying to remember all the things he told me about his mother, dog, work, friends, garden, gerbil, tomato plants, and then I'd meet him and realize I couldn't tell from his photo that he actually looks like my great Uncle Melvin who always gave me the creeps, and the whole thing was a colossal waste of time.

Which brings me to Stage Three. This stage occurs when Stage Two has careened to a screeching halt. Because it DOES NOT WORK. You simply must invest a *bit* of time. Stage Three = Common Sense or Middle Ground. You have to dig a little deeper. Exchange a few emails. Have a long enough phone call to ascertain some commonality of interests and humor. And, it doesn't hurt, at all, to check that he has several (the more the better) pictures of himself on the site. The reasons for this will become clear.

Bear in mind, that for the next man I am going to tell you about, I was now firmly in Stage Two. I had exchanged an email or two with a guy named Greg, who seemed OK, dare I say normal, during our first phone call.

Greg had only posted one photo, but it showed an attractive man, with dark wavy hair, and a slightly crooked smile that carried warmth and self-deprecation (I imagined). He listened well and had a fun sense of humor on our short phone chat. So, when he suggested we meet quickly, not talk for ages, I agreed to a coffee date the next day. Hmmm, will this one go any better than the others?

I found the coffee shop in Greenwich easily enough. This time, I had wised up – it was a Saturday late morning and the traffic was not a killer.

Greenwich is such a gorgeous town, with a beautiful central street of gift shops, art galleries, boutiques, and bistros. It is one of those rare towns left on the planet that boasts a coffee shop to compete with and rival Starbucks. Now I have nothing against Starbucks, but it is taking over the world, don't you think? The money that company must have made off internet dating! It is *the* place to meet.

By the way, and as an aside, how on earth did that company ever persuade us to pay almost four dollars for a cup of coffee with some foamy, airy milk in it? How did they do that? You have to give them credit for marketing, PR, cahoneys, or something.

I arrived first, and after checking my makeup in the rear view mirror, I went in and found a table. The coffee shop was unassuming, with small wooden tables and chairs, big glass windows, and lots of newspapers and magazines lying around. I picked up a New York Times someone had left behind and tried to read an article on global warming, while surreptitiously watching the door. As usual, I was doing the "trying to look cool while furtively checking out each person that comes in" drill, and for a brief instant hoping (or not hoping) that each new guy was the man I was there to meet.

I smiled at myself. I still believed it would be easy. Newbie that I was, I thought how hard could it be to meet someone nice, and at least have a friendship, someone to go to the movies with.

I didn't know the ropes. However, I learned them. Oh, I learned them. Now, years later, I know a few things. For example, rarely do people look like the photo they have put up online. *Rarely.* If the photo looks just great, and everything about him nails you between the eyes, it will somehow just *not* be there when he is there in the flesh. He will almost always be shorter, fatter and older.

And, the reverse can sometimes be true. A perfectly handsome man can be non-photogenic, and then when you meet him you are pleasantly surprised. Unfortunately, this is rarely the case.

As I waited at the table, I saw a man come through the door, look around, and spot me. Recognition brightened into a smile. He headed toward me.

Wait a minute. Is that *him*? How could that be him? If that was indeed his picture on the site, it must have been taken 20 years and 20 pounds ago. Or, it was of a GQ model. Or his roommate in college. While his roommate was *in* college.

But, then again, hang on, he did look a *little* like the photo... Perhaps a family resemblance. Was the picture of his kid brother?

As we met, shook hands, did the jacket off, coffee-buying thing, the whole time I couldn't shake the feeling that I was talking to someone he had sent in his place.

Not knowing what to do, I chatted as merrily as I could manage, I asked questions, and figured I'd learn more about him before I passed judgment. (What a novel thought, Laura...)

I was funny, bright, scintillating (I think), but I discovered that we didn't have much in common. He was involved with some fund or other, Wall Street talk I only partially understood, and he had no interest in alternative medicine. Why was I here again?

I found myself getting annoyed, with myself, mostly. Why did I jump into this?

But, I was annoyed with him, too. A little voice in me kept whining, "This is bait and switch. He cheated. This is not *fair*."

In any event, I knew from the first few moments that there was no way I was going to see this man again.

Just to show you how poorly this meeting was going, I longed to be home. The bathroom floor needed scrubbing. Yes, it did.

After 20 minutes or so of shallow, forced chatter, (on my part anyway), I figured I had done enough, and could make tracks. If I couldn't get away easily, I held at the ready such excuses as: "This was fun, it was nice to meet you, but I simply must get on home and feed the cat, water the plants, wash my hair, write a screenplay." Or, I could always bring up the 400 orphaned children who needed me desperately...

I suppressed a grin.

I began the gracious, I-need-to-get-going noises.

His response was startling, to say the least. He burst out, "This has been fabulous. I knew I'd find you if I looked long enough. You are it. You are the one."

He grinned happily.

I was rendered speechless, but he didn't seem to notice any discomfiture on my part.

He exclaimed, "I think we should move in together as soon as possible and we can get married whenever you like."

Should I be flattered he had reacted so positively to me? Uh, no. Clearly, this man was insane. A touch of fear for my safety flashed through me.

He continued, "I can't believe I've found you. I don't have to look any more."

I stared, and muttered, "Uh...."

He plowed on.

"I think you are wonderful, just perfect, and I'm so glad I got on Match. My friends told me to and I didn't want to do it. Oh wow, I've found you!"

Of course I would have thought he was joking if I hadn't been there, seen his face, his sincerity. It flashed through my mind: how was I going to get to my car without this crazy person following me?

I mumbled something relatively incoherent, along the lines of, "That's amazing you feel this way so quickly," and he was off again.

"I haven't felt this way for years, didn't know it could happen again for me! You are it, you the one. You are *it.*"

"*It.*" There it was again. The word hung in the air. My mystified mind chose that moment to conjure up Cousin Itt, from the *Adams Family*. A three-foot-tall creature, all hair and feet and a hat.

Odd as it was, Cousin Itt seemed far more credible than the strange male person sitting across from me, now. This man seemed to have absolutely no recognition that I was not reciprocating. I was not feeling the same things, not having the same thoughts... Not even in the same room any longer. There might have been a brief puff of dust as I hurtled for the door, raced to my trusty little Honda CRV and tore off, before he could even react, or follow me. I heard him call my name, and his surprised protestations as the door slammed behind me.

But, I didn't feel even slightly guilty, or even rude. I just knew that sometimes you just have to take an opportunity to run for your life.

Chapter 4

You're Already Gone

"I see when men love women. They give them but a little of their lives. But women when they love give everything."
~ Oscar Wilde

The next day I called Francesca and shared the story of my coffee date with Greg. Strange, inexplicable Greg. Who talked marriage after 20 minutes with me. Every time I thought about it, I couldn't believe it.

"You know," I said, "I've been thinking about this crazy guy I met last night... Nobody, I mean *nobody* meets someone and asks them to marry him that same moment. I mean, seriously?"

"It is a little odd," she said.

"Maybe it was a bit clever. Maybe he hated me, knew immediately it wouldn't work, and this was his way of making sure I wouldn't pursue him..."

I heard a guffaw.

"Nope," she replied. "No way, babe, he was just bowled over by you and couldn't help himself."

"You are the dearest woman, but... I. Don't. Think. So."

She laughed. "I have a suggestion. You open to that?"

"Sure."

"There's something wrong with all of them."

"Excuse me?"

"Yup. As you meet these guys, try reminding yourself of that. It will help you to bring your expectations down a little. It's simple: There's something wrong with all of them."

I chuckled. "Even Keith?"

"Oh, God, no," she replied. "He's perfect." Sarcasm drizzled through the phone line.

Hmmm, I thought. I waited for her to elaborate, but she didn't.

Oh, my God, is it that simple? Is it true? Is there something wrong with all of them? Men, I mean?

"Of course, we women, on the other hand, are misunderstood, loving, angel-people," I said.

"Uh-huh," Francesca said.

In truth, yes, there is something wrong with every one of us, male and female, I guess. The moment arrives in any new relationship where you decide whether or not you can deal with what is wrong with the other. I guess they are deciding if they can deal with what is wrong with you. Or not.

"The list of things wrong with Kurt would fill a giant tome. Anyway, it doesn't matter. I think I am done with men." I know I sounded derisive, cynical, hopeless.

"Yeah, right, Laura, good luck with that."

♦ ♦ ♦

Ah, Kurt, (aka Mr. Callous and Incredibly Adept Liar. Oh, that's not a name? Should be.) I'd met him in a bookstore in the spirituality/self-help section. We got talking. I got lucky. Well, with hindsight, maybe not.

He was tall, dark, handsome and sexy. (Throw in a quarter cup of loser, but I didn't know that, then). He nailed me between the eyes. Within a few months, I thought he was the love of my life. Seven years later, I would have thrown myself in front of a bus if it would save him.

I once described to Francesca how it felt, what it was like for me with Kurt. We were trying a test I'd seen online – must have been on *Oprah* or *Cosmo* or somewhere. You were to ask yourself this question: If you had 30 seconds to live, because a meteorite was going to hit your house, whose face would you like to see in the last moment of your life? Whose eyes would you want to be looking into? For me it was Kurt, almost from the moment we met.

No one had broken my heart before Kurt. I'd made it all the way to 45 years old without getting my heart broken. Can you believe that? My first boyfriend, in my twenties, was an alcoholic. Irish. Gorgeous. But, drank, oh my God, did he drink. Hidden bottles of scotch all over the place. Behind the bureau. In with the spare tire in the car. Behind planters in the garden shed. I loved him, he was such a great guy in so many ways. Kind, funny, very talented. But, I couldn't take the alcohol. After a couple of years, I finally announced that it was the drink, or me. Yup, I know what you're thinking. You're right. He chose the drink.

I was sad and worried for him, but it didn't break my heart in the way we think of it. I wasn't devastated.

My second long-term relationship – I was 28 or 29... Nutshell, he cheated on me. Only once. Someone only cheats on me once. I remember the way I found out. A hotel clerk called to say he had failed to sign the credit card form, or something, and could he call the hotel immediately. Ha ha. I called him where he was away on business and he was full of lame excuses. Oh, he sputtered and told me that some colleague of his was staying in the hotel, and his company had bought him the hotel room for the night, and hadn't signed. On and on and on. Defensive and over-compensating all over the place. The jerk.

But, oddly, that didn't break my heart. You'd think it would, right? He cheated on me. But, I knew I didn't love him in the way other people talked about love. We got along well, and so it just worked on some level. But, I had never felt much in the way of any passion.

I realized, then, that I just didn't care. It was an excuse to break up, in actual fact.

Then there was Kurt. Oh, yes, Kurt.

Where did I go wrong? He just stopped loving me. How do you do that? If you do truly love somebody, can you just stop one day? These thoughts go trundling around and around your brain again, even while you are trying to move forward. Or, they did in mine.

Did I give myself away? Did I lose myself? When he had dumped the whole "I don't know if I love you anymore" line on me, why on earth didn't I tell him, right then and there, to jump straight in the nearest stagnant pond? Never mind that this was the love of my life, why didn't I just take a deep breath and tell him to look me up when he'd figured it out and we'd see if I was still interested? But, I doubt I would be.

Ba bing. Zap, take that, ya bugger.

Why did I say pathetic things like, "When will you know for sure?" and "How can I help?" and "Let's go have therapy together."

No, instead, I waited, patiently, staring in vain through a three-inch glass wall he had built between us. A wall of ice, was more like it. I could see him, but I couldn't reach him. I couldn't feel him. I lay there in bed, next to him, night after night, the sheets feeling so cold. I felt lonelier than if I were alone. Have you ever felt like that? Worse than being alone.

This was truly a prolific time for my poetry writing. I intended someday to put them to music. In the meantime, it was always a cathartic experience. In the horrible months after he walked away the floodgates opened.

Marianne Faithfull once said, "Maybe the most that you can expect from a relationship that goes bad is to come out of it with a few good songs."

You're Already Gone

Looking at you
through a 3-inch wall
of ice and tears
Looking right through
as the days stretched into years
Would it make any difference
if I wait for you?

You're already gone.

I can see you
but can't touch you at all.
I cry out to you,
but you don't hear my call.
You've withdrawn to a distance
where I can't even go.
You're already gone

I've taken your hand,
and given you my all.
Done everything I can
to shatter that wall.
I'd pray forever
if you'd come back to me.
But you're already gone.
You're already gone.

I had a dream that night. Kurt had left a giant baked ham (you know the ones, honey-soaked heaven...) in a warming oven. Not a regular heat level for baking – that would dry it out or burn it. No, it just stayed warm. This meant it wasn't hot enough to keep it safe, just hot enough to encourage all those happy little bacteria lurking in the meat to spoil it, fast. And he had clearly forgotten and left it there, for hours.

The sensation, the emotion, in the dream was powerful: I was so angry and irritated by the loss, the sheer tragedy of it all. How careless he had been to waste such a perfect ham, so nourishing, so delectable to us both. He just let it sit there and rot, without making any effort to save it. He'd forgotten all about it.

The message was so obvious as to make me groan when I woke up. It hung over me for hours, the awareness that I still loved a man who could be that careless.

And I really, really missed the ham.

Chapter 5

Dropping Pebbles

*"I've been on so many blind dates,
I should get a free dog."*
~ Wendy Liebman

Online dating. Here we go again. No wait a minute, I need to... there must be *something* I need to do.

I had finished with my preparations for clients I would see the next day, eaten a simple dinner of wild salmon and Basmati rice (I did look after myself most of the time... OK, some of the time), had cleaned up the kitchen, cleaned out the kitty litter box, faithfully trekked around the townhouse complex, made my cup of decaf tea... There wasn't anything else I could think of to do to put it off any longer. Except maybe call my mother, and that item was always way down the list of things I wanted to do. That was even harder work than online dating.

I suppose I could always rotate the tires on my Honda. Wait a minute. I don't know how to rotate tires. Sigh. If I only had a man.

Ha!

I took a deep breath. And settled back down at the computer. I can do this. As it came up out of hibernation, I mused.

I acknowledge that online dating is a weird phenomenon. You surf across a thousand men on various personals sites, automatically eliminating 90% of them for not meeting your specific criteria (or for a plethora of imagined failings). For example, you can leave out all men under 5 feet, 8 inches (all men lie about their height). Or maybe you only want to see men that list themselves as either "athletic" or "slender" (all men lie about their physique). Or, you can spend five minutes pounding your forehead on the keyboard and see what that brings you.

You can hone it down to a single or divorced male, between 5'10" and 6'5," college educated, living within 50 miles of Fairfield, Connecticut, with a "fit" or slender physique. One who is politically moderate, and "spiritual not religious." That is exactly what I did. There were 647 of them on Match that day. 647 men. Now there's an overwhelming thought. Especially when you consider that 639 of them were 5'2", built like the Pillsbury Doughboy, and lived in their mom's basement.

I closed my laptop.

But wait, I guess I liken it to a prizefight. Each time the bell rings, you've got to get back out there. Keep doing it. The odds are working against you so you have to put the time in. Take the punches and come back ready, bruises and concussions be damned.

I opened my laptop again.

Why do we think it should be easy? Remember grade school? When there were a hundred kids or more you knew in your grade? How many of them did you like? Maybe one? (The only one I remember is Bruce, a funny, smart, confident 8-year-old hunk for whom I pined in the third grade. Of course, he didn't know I existed.)

However, if you remember those numbers when you are sifting through the hundreds (or thousands) of available people on online dating sites, it helps. There were tons of kids in your grade, and the odds were incredibly small you would take a shine to one of them.

So, with online dating, that makes the odds one in a hundred? Perhaps one in a thousand? Who knows? How many cups of coffee is that? Sigh.

Drop a pebble in a lake
and watch the waters part
Till the rings reach every shore around
and touch some other heart

I stand here at the water's edge
praying for a sign
that somewhere out across the mist
there beats a heart like mine

Maybe there's an answer
Maybe you'll set me free
Maybe you'll drop a pebble
and warm the heart in me

Ok, so I must drop more pebbles.

I signed into Match and ramped up some determination. Online dating does work, I reminded myself. You can actually meet someone nice, make a friend, and meet an honest person who truly wants a good relationship.

However, and I apologize if I am throwing a skunk on the picnic table, you'll just have to do some knee-deep wading. Sometimes that wading is through knee-deep *muck,* though.

I met Henry, my accountant, online. A great guy and I wanted like anything for it to work. The attraction was there, he was kind, good looking, and had a wonderful little Maine coon cat named Mitzy who I adored. But, we didn't have enough in common to sustain a relationship. Here's an example: he loathed gardening, and wanted to spend the rest of his life playing golf. I think golf is a waste of green space. Or as Mark Twain put it, "Golf is a good walk ruined." 'Nuff said.

After half a dozen friendly dates, he hesitantly said, over dinner, "You know, Laura, we aren't soul mates."

"I know," I said. The realization had made me sad. I wondered if I even had one, or if I did, whether I would find him this lifetime. Before I was too old to give a damn.

Henry and I agreed to be friends. We have remained so. (And you *know* I didn't want to go find another accountant.)

I also met my dear friend, Hank, online. We recognized each other as kindred spirits from the moment we met. The first evening we got together, we gabbed merrily over dinner, for hours, in a little Thai restaurant in Danbury until they shooed us out so they could close up. Don't you just love those evenings? They are pretty rare.

However, as for the two of us being an item? Well, he was recovering from the breakup of his long-term relationship, and I was recovering from a divorce...Wait, but you were both on dating sites, I hear you exclaim. Well, first of all, sometimes there is simply no rhyme or reason to things. But that's not good enough. I will offer up this defense: many people on dating sites are not ready. I certainly wasn't, and maybe I was using online dating as de facto therapy. Or more to the point, the way to get over one guy is to get under another. Sounds great, but I hadn't tried that one yet.

Anyway, Hank and I, as a potential couple, just didn't feel... *right*. The chemistry wasn't there, or we felt more like brother and sister, or something. We actually had the presence of mind to recognize we would be better as friends.

He was a talented photographer, incredibly smart, spiritual, and funny as hell. I have never had such a good male friend. Like a brother. And so good-looking – he looked like a young Christopher Plummer.

We didn't suit each other very well for lifelong partners. I'm a little too glamorous. I am a girlie-girl, I admit it. I like nail polish and jewelry; he likes camping out on the beach in the sand dunes of the New Jersey shore. He once told me his favorite sexy image is of a beautiful girl, naked, with just hiking boots on. I like classical music, soft country, oldies rock and roll. He likes incomprehensible jazz that makes me dizzy and irritated. Our minds work alike, but our tastes and lifestyles don't.

The phone rang, saving me from more online searching. Or soul-searching.

It was Hank. Speak of the devil.

"Hey, Hank!"

Hank often called me on his way home from his studio. There was a dead zone around the wilds of Easton as he headed back to his home in Newtown, but we got used to it and worked around it.

"Hey, gorgeous. You ready for tomorrow?" Hank had told me of his plan to hike to the summit of Race Mountain, in southern Massachusetts, before it got too cold. He had managed to finagle me into going with him. I had even agreed to spend 150 bucks on a new pair of hiking boots. Plus, I assured him I could easily carry a 25-pound backpack. Oh, my, what a fool I could be.

"I've been running up and down the stairs ten times a day for a week, if that's what you mean," I replied.

"Damn straight. Good for you."

"And I'm still wading through profiles on Match. Working my way through all these guys."

He replied, quick as a flash, "They're hoping to work their way through you, too."

While I was still laughing he added, "And I envy all of them."

What a sweetheart.

Chapter 6

Escape to Race Mountain

*It isn't the mountains ahead to climb that wear you out;
it's the pebble in your shoe.*
~ Muhammad Ali

Hank and I met at nine the next morning, on a warm, even muggy day, early in September. We grabbed egg sandwiches at a wonderful little country store before we began our tromp up the hillside.

He had hiked up Race Mountain, one of the larger mountains in southwestern Massachusetts, many times. On the Appalachian Trail, it was a beautiful, if exhausting (for me), trek. Four or five hours more or less straight up, past three exquisite waterfalls and many breathtaking views across vast expanses of wooded and mountainous countryside. The plan was to stay the night in the tent he carried, and then come down the next morning.

When we'd been climbing for two hours up the mountain, it began to slowly dawn on me that Race Mountain was a lot taller than the stairs in my townhouse. There was pain and exhaustion in store.

But, we had so much fun! This was a little odd, considering:

1) I had to walk with the laces unfastened most of the way because my new boots hurt like the very devil. Those brand new, expensive hiking boots had torn silver-dollar-sized holes in the back of my ankles.

2) We plopped down the tent over lovely deep grasses, flattening and crushing them in the process. I am allergic to wheat, which is a grain. Grasses are grains. That math added up to a sneeze-fest. A sneeze marathon. I sneezed all evening, all night, and the next morning I resembled a red-eyed, puffy-faced, sniveling alien.

3) The pack was heavy, I was not that fit, and every bit of me started to hurt. Late that night, lying in the tent on the hard ground, I tried to find one little area, one miniscule portion of my body that was pain-free. I hunted for a place to focus my mind that did not hold an ache of some sort. Right thumb seemed to be OK... Thank goodness for wee blessings.

4) Creeping out of the tent to pee in the middle of the night, I hung my butt out in the night air, did my business, and got three mosquito bites on my cheeks in the same number of minutes. But, I tried to look on the bright side; it wasn't poison ivy!

Hank decided my new name should be "Warrior Woman," for enduring all of this. I thought it was a bit much, but it sounded complementary and impressive, so I didn't argue.

Here is the truly good stuff. Warm for September, I cooled off in my undies under the waterfalls we discovered all the way up Race Mountain. You have heard the list of encumbrances and aches and sneezes and bites on the butt. But, oh, the views! The clean mountain air, the smoked salmon, the meat seared over an open fire! Figure in Hank's hilarious observations on everything from other hikers to me in my undies under the waterfall, and the whole trip was a blast.

He'd marinated steak, potatoes, and peppers in a yummy Italian dressing and carried them all the way up the mountain. Then he made a small fire under the stars and cooked this concoction. Oh, heaven. I was starving!

Later we gazed up at more stars than I knew existed, and felt like tiny ants at the top of a mountain overlooking the panorama of Connecticut and Massachusetts laid out before us. Endless miles of forests and hills, with only the distant lights of a few scattered towns reminding us of civilization.

"Do you believe in God?" I asked suddenly, out of nowhere. The view inspired this kind of question. There just had to be a God to create a world so beautiful.

"Yes, but not in the external sense of a God that you pray to, to help you find a parking spot."

I chuckled and nodded.

He said, "Prayer is such a waste of time. God created all this, gave us free will, and left us to get on with it."

I nodded. "My friend David says, 'I believe there is a God. I just don't think he plans his day around me.'"

"Oh, good one!" Hank laughed. "And where are you with all that?"

"The online dating sites give you choices when it comes to religion. Obviously all the Christian denominations, Baptist, Episcopalian, etc. And Buddhist, Hindu.... Or 'Spiritual, not Religious.' I check off that one."

As we reveled in the glory that was that view, I told Hank a little of my journey. My spiritual path, or self-awareness and consciousness focus, or whatever you want to call it, all started with some therapy, years before. The therapist put *The Road Less Traveled* into my hand (thank you, endlessly, Dr. Scott Peck). I was hooked and have been on some sort of self-discovery/spiritual path ever since. From Eckhart Tolle to Wayne Dyer, from Pema Chodron to the Dalai Lama, I had read everything in this genre I could get my hands on.

I understand it: the focus on loving, kindness, forgiving, gratitude, the whole staying-in-the-moment thing, the advantages of a Zen-like, middle ground of emotion.

But, and it is a big old but, I don't manage to stay with it during the trials and tribulations of life, I'm afraid. And, that's when you need it! The goal may be the ability to objectify, to step outside of one's emotions to look at them, thereby freeing you of their clutch. But, it's hard. Worth it when you figure out how to do it, I guess. The books all lay it out as if it is so damned simple. "God and peace is within you..." Yeah, yeah, yeah, how's that been working out for you, Laura?

How do you remember that, live from that belief, when there is no peace in your life? When someone cheats on you, lies to you, hurts you? When you are in a state of grief? You dive into therapy, thinking there must be something wrong with you. Yup, your self-worth takes another hit. You don't want the damage to form an iron casement around your heart.

But, do we have control over that? When you lose any sense of being sure of yourself, what do you do to regain that?

I'd have given a lot to know the answers to those questions.

So, back to Race Mountain. After a night of sneezing, laughing with Hank, and swatting mosquitoes, I finally drifted into an exhausted sleep about four a.m.

Five minutes later, he woke me up to see the incredible dawn, which he swore on his mother's life I absolutely could not miss.

I groaned. "You're lucky I like you…"

Turned out he was right. He put a cup of coffee in my hand (how on earth had he pulled that off?) and led me to the edge of the huge flat rocks that graced the top of Race Mountain. And there it was, the first sunrise ever. The red and gold streaks across the vast open sky were like nothing I had ever seen before. It took my breath away. I wanted to capture the image in a photo, but knew, somehow, that it would never suffice. There were no words, either. We stood silently, for some time, taking in that wonder.

We talked about the dating thing while we scrambled back down the hill to head home. Of course, this was about *my* dating thing, since he had decided to bag the whole thing forever.

"My heart can't take anymore," he said.

I said, "Yes, well, it's harder, I think, as we get older. Our options recede, somewhat…"

He nodded. "Along with the hairline, our gums, and the chances of getting laid."

I told him about all the guys, and winking, and crazy brief dates with strange people. I chuckled as I explained that guys were dropping like flies all over the place.

"Oh, man," he replied, "what an image...."

He took a couple of long swigs from his water bottle.

"I have this great picture: you, standing at your kitchen window, and the sill beneath you is strewn with dead flies... Most of them are as dead as mackerels, but one or two of them are on their backs, their legs are moving, and they are buzzing from time to time."

He handed me the water bottle, and went on, "A couple more flies are creeping out from between the glass and the wall, but you have a trusty *People* magazine rolled up that'll take care of them."

I laughed until my face hurt.

We had managed *not* to talk about our lost loves, for this trip, having vowed that we could achieve whole two days without pining or whining.

◆ ◆ ◆

When I got home, I was more tired than I could ever remember being. That night, after a long Epsom Salts bath, I climbed into my toaster oven. I had an electric blanket above me, and a mattress warmer under me, underneath the bottom sheet. I turned them both on high for an hour or two before bed, then turned them off and slid in, groaning in ecstasy. Even on a mild September evening the sheets were cold, but not with a toaster oven. All muscles turned instantly to molasses...

I fell into a deep, deep sleep. Fresh air and that amount of exertion will do that to you.

In the middle of the night, I dreamt of Kurt again. We were in a plane, which suddenly went up and over itself in a gigantic loop. Then headed down. Down! Panic seared through me. Then, I was suddenly transported outside of the plane for an instant. Staring back at all those windows, I saw, but did not hear, the screams of each face looking out, clutching at the window.

Then, just as suddenly, I was back in my seat with the cold, jagged truth washing over me. We were going down. We were going to die. I looked over at Kurt, and asked, "Is this it?"

He turned and looked at me blankly for a moment.

"I love you," I said, feeling naked, vulnerable, my heart on display.

He didn't say it back. He didn't even look at me again, but turned to the window. I waited, each second feeling like an eternity.

I said, "I don't want to die. I hope it doesn't hurt too much... I guess we will be gone in an instant, and not feel a thing."

He said nothing, just continued to stare out of the window.

Just as I thought the fear was going to choke me, the plane pulled up, leveled out, and everything slowly returned to normal.

I woke up, drenched in sweat, my heart pounding double time, and tears in my eyes.

He hadn't said it back to me. He didn't even know at the moment of death whether he loved me or not. He didn't say it back.

Now, I knew this on some level in my waking hours, but denial is a marvelous thing. I had spent two years trying to pretend that he did still love me, that everything would be fine if I could just wait it out. It was just a mid-life crisis, or he had shoved his feelings down under the suit of armor he wore to protect himself from hurt. And, I could be patient and wait.

But, the dreaming Laura knew the truth, and had chosen an exquisite way to club me over the head with it. He didn't love me anymore. What was it going to take for me to understand? How long could I stay in denial?

Francesca kept asking me, "What part of him moving 250 miles away don't you get?"

I had to concede the point.

Chapter 7

I'm So Past Some Good-Looking Guy

Ever tried. Ever failed. No matter. Try Again.
Fail again. Fail better.
~ Samuel Beckett

    I had learned quite a bit about online dating by this time. First of all, the guy is expected to give the phone number out to the woman – in this case, to me. That way I could block my number on his Caller ID. I could "vet" him a little before giving my private phone number. Or my private email outside of the Match inbox. Sometimes, I made it all the way to that first cup of coffee without the gent having any idea how to reach me. Believe me, I was grateful I'd withheld. On more than one occasion.

    One particularly horrible coffee date went so far south that I drove in circles around the coffee house to make sure he wasn't following me. I waved at people in the window of that same shop 17 times as I drove by, again and again... They say if you think you're being followed, make three left turns in a row, because nobody who's ever trying to get anywhere does that. If he's still behind you, head for the police station.

Oh my.

On that note, if you're serious about privacy and security, you can make use of another tool a friend suggested to me: you can get a cheap track or burner phone, which you set up with voice mail. But you never answer it! That is the number I gave out, at first, so I could hear his voice when he left a message, and he didn't know this was not my private number.

One problem, however. One guy and I traded calls for weeks before I figured out he was doing the same thing. It fizzled out. Nobody talked to anybody, and at some point, one of us must have realized we just didn't care. That was the end of that. It's been years, and he still hasn't found anyone. Maybe it's because I still occasionally leave him a message, just to mess with his head.

Hee hee... only kidding.

So here I was, once again, scrolling through profiles online. For hours. For months. Was I going to do this for the rest of my life? It felt like it, sometimes.

Then suddenly, I was stopped in my tracks by a truly beautiful face. Is that a weird thing to say about a man? Not really. *He was just beautiful.* And not in an effeminate way. Light brown wavy hair, and a full beard and mustache, which I've always loved. I think it is a grave oversight on the part of those women who do not appreciate wonderful whiskers.

Oh my, he had such a handsome face. His articulate and interesting profile revealed a talented graphic designer, and I clicked on the link he provided to view some of his artwork and designs. An intelligent, creative guy! And he didn't live far away.

Things were looking up!

I could feel the first tiny tremors of hope rising. I quickly tried to squash them utterly, and not be tempted to believe again.

Thus began something of an eye-opener.

The requisite first phone conversation went pretty well, although he was rather serious, and I'd always wanted someone who could make me laugh. Like Kurt. He could always have me in stitches, as he had such an absurd take on things. He'd say something outrageous, and as I was laughing, he'd carry on painting an ever more hilarious and ridiculous picture, on and on, getting more and more implausible. Early on in the relationship, I said to him, "Stop, come back, you've gone to North Carolina." Some days he'd get as far as South Carolina, and I remember one particularly extravagant time when I swear he got all the way to Florida. At the beginning of lovemaking, sometimes he'd launch into one of these creative tales. I'd laugh until I was wiping my eyes. I had to bring his focus back to me by tapping on his shoulder and with my best lisp, say "Hey Mithter, focuth – thtay with me, focuth."

We'd laugh so hard it would take a while to get back to the business at hand.

Ah, Kurt...

Now, now, enough, Laura.

In my phone call with Mr. Handsome, there were no examples of his sense of humor, but I certainly wasn't going to write him off. We both played finger-picking acoustic guitar and liked a lot of the same music. He shared the same loathing of politicians. We heartily bemoaned the mess Congress was in.

There was some promise in this intriguing man and we'd find humor when we got together. I would see to it! Being a goofball, I can usually make most anyone laugh, if I care to. So Mr. Handsome and I made a plan to meet Friday evening for coffee and we were off and rolling.

It's a weird and wonderful path on the way to the first meeting. There is hope, a hope which experience teaches you to underplay. You get pretty damned tired, pretty damned soon, of spending a week or two or three dreaming and fantasizing about how this is going to be the big one, the right one. That you might find the real love of your life. You play up all the good qualities you have learned about the person, and don't yet know any of the negative. Everyone has been promoting their good stuff, as you'd expect in any advertising medium, so of course you haven't had a chance to find out any of the startling array of peoples' disappointing flaws.

Eventually, you learn to downplay your expectations. As wise Francesca suggested.

Nevertheless, hope has a way of bobbing to the surface like a cheerful little orange duck in the bathtub, and although you try to shove it down, it pops back up. This goes on for however many hours or days there are until the first meeting.

Unfortunately, the vast majority of first meetings are a screaming disappointment. It is usually a little like looking forward to a movie that has garnered rave reviews everywhere, and you've looked forward to seeing it. Then, on the night, you hate it, and oddly, you hate it even more because you feel all those critics are idiots, or they ripped you off somehow. Like when I saw *The English Patient* that reviewers raved about, and waited for three hours for the happy redemptive ending. Ha ha ha on me. Oh, was I pissed! Or "*Howard's End*," which I have since renamed, "*When Is it Ever Going to End.*"

Maybe that's why online dating holds so much in the way of disappointment. When you meet someone at a party, you probably arrived there without an expectation in the world. So, happening on someone interesting with whom you find chemistry is a rare and delightful surprise!

When I arrived at Starbucks, Mr. Handsome was already there, waiting for me, in one of those big lumpy brown chairs they sometimes have at coffee places.

Wow, is he ever gorgeous, I thought to myself. After the first few minutes of getting lattes, hanging up coats, and all that business, we settled in.

"Why did you move up here from the city?" I asked.

"My mom got sick... Dad needed some help to look after her, and I figured I could run my graphic design business just as well from up here. At least for a while. And it is easy to hop on a train and get down there to meet potential new clients."

"Hmmm," I said, "that's quite a change. What's it like being with your parents so much? You're not living with them?"

"Oh, no," he said quickly.

"I couldn't deal with that, I confess... I might kill my mother in less than 48 hours if I had to live with her again. I wouldn't mean to, it would just come down to it. Can't Help. My. Self.'"

He chuckled and nodded. "No, I found a great apartment in SoNo."

I looked blankly at him.

"Oh, SoNo," he said, "short for South Norwalk."

"Ah, right" I said, the light bulb going off. I remembered a client telling me about SoNo, which he explained was a cool, "happening" place, as she put it. I guess I wasn't very cool or happening. Singles bars, clubs, and expensive eateries were not my thing, somehow.

So, Mr. Handsome and I had learned that we shared an exhausting inability to get along with our mothers. Then we went on to explore each other's histories and viewpoints. We railed against Wall Street, the banks, Congress, the Middle East, agreeing the world seemed to have abandoned all reason. We even got into some metaphysical stuff – the meaning of life and love.

As I sat across from Mr. Handsome Manhattan, I was listening, nodding, uttering nice encouraging things, and silently saying, "Damn, is he good looking."

But, there was another part of me – the Laura I needed to hear from. I waited. I leaned back into my chair, and I found myself hunting inside for some sort of internal reaction to this man, other than the very mental and objective valuation of how gorgeous he was. I looked for some slight flutter, some bit of turn on, some chunk of excitement, anticipation, or nerves. All those things I used to feel... like the old days, before that horrible moment in the kitchen.

Instead, there was a long silence from Inner Laura.

Wait a minute here, girl, couldn't I even view it as a great weekend romp, a roll in the proverbial, a good servicing, a great "seeing to"? Still silence.

Then Inner Laura whispered back a single line as a message to my conscious.

"I don't give a shit."

Nope. It seems like I was just so past some good-looking guy.

Chapter 8

It Must Be Me

"I can trust my friends. These people force me to examine myself, encourage me to grow."
~ Cher

After the disenchantment of my coffee date with Mr. Handsome, I knew it must be me. I must be completely dead inside. Because if I couldn't get interested in that handsome hunk, I must be seriously unwell in some way.

Was there a hospital, a treatment, a doctor, for a broken-down woman who couldn't even recognize something good when it was sitting in front of her?

Then, driving home, I realized something. A bit of an "ah-ha" moment. The truth was, I didn't trust myself anymore. Didn't trust my judgment. It was bad enough not knowing who I would meet, or how to get a sense of them, or who to trust. If you doubt *yourself*, and the way you have always done things, you're on shaky ground. This is off-putting, to say the least.

I was facing the unwelcome notion that I had been giving myself away in my relationships with men. When you get together with someone in a relationship, ideally you climb into a new car, take off on an all-new joint path, and you take turns driving.... Ideally. This has not always been the case in my own life, I'm afraid.

I love the way Hank put it to me.

"Have you ever thought that you are not even living your own life, you're just creeping in and out of a chapter of someone else's life?" he asked.

Ouch. Holy Moly. He hit it on the head. I paid attention and tried to take this to heart. In and out of a chapter of other people's lives. That's what I'd done, I'd fit myself into other people's lives. And then came the bigger realization. Wait a cotton pickin' minute, no one had ever fitted themselves into *my* life. Except the guy who services my car.

This is more commonly a woman thing, I think, don't you? Men seem to find it easier to stay straight and true to themselves. More easily than we do. They announce who they are, what they want, their goals and dreams, and women so often fit into that. I hope younger women are not as guilty of this as we are.

I have always had a theory about relationships. I call it the "Leaning Theory." Hold your hands up in front of your face, palms facing each other. Imagine this is you and your partner. If your right hand moves away, the left hand often follows it to maintain proximity, closeness. This can be a mistake! Soon, one hand is flat and the other is squashing it... So, my theory is that when one partner pulls away a little, give him space! He will come find you. You hope. Or, your right hand can grab a brick and beat your left hand to a pulp with it.

The only problem with this is you have to be incredibly sure of yourself. Your self-worth has to be strong, intact, undamaged, and you have to be *brave*. And have a lifetime supply of bricks.

I could feel myself sinking into a pit. Maybe it's all hopeless, really. Nothing will ever work out and it's pointless to try. When I get like this, I think weird, sad thoughts, and should simply be slapped up side the head. Thoughts like: maybe the truth is that God is a cat, playing with me... I am that poor, sad mouse. He has not even decided to kill me off yet, he has just walked away, left me half dead and dying, and has lost interest.

Uh-oh. I realized I needed help. Maybe I should go to a therapist again – I needed to talk it out. It had been almost five months since Kurt slithered out, and I should be doing much better, shouldn't I?

I sent an email to Hank, telling him the story of Mr. Handsome. At the end of my email, I told him all I could do was think of Kurt. I said, in fact, I was at the peak of lows.

Here is his reply:

Sorry for you and your peak of lows. I wish there was a spiritual Viagra pill out there somewhere, something you could just pop and get hugely excited about life again...
But, hey, it could be worse.
♦ You could have an alarm clock that wakes you in the morning with spit.
♦ You could be rear-ended by a truck, and when they try to take you to the hospital, you refuse, since you know you are wearing your oldest bra that has a hole in it.

♦ *You could discover that the artificial ivy you have hanging in the foyer has an artificial fungus, and must be thrown out.*
♦ *The handsomest man you've ever seen watched you pick your nose at a red light. He looks away. You wish you were dead.*
♦ *Your new puppy left a pile on the carpet, and the Roomba found it before you did.*
♦ *You could suddenly realize that your car is aggressively ugly. Why didn't you see that before?*
♦ *You could discover that every investment of time and energy that you've ever made in your entire life is returned, postage due.*
♦ *The breadcrumbs you cast on the waters begin to kill the fish.*

"Hank," you cry out, "I just want to be happy." But, at the moment you say it, I'm thinking pepperoni pizza and a beer sound real good, so I nod sympathetically, and ask you if you have any napkins.

Ah, Laura, these cards have been dealt before. There are not that many cards in the deck, so they undoubtedly have been dealt before.

Our choices:
1. Hate the bastards that always seem to be winning, but probably have hearts the size of mothballs and dream in black and white.
2. Leave this weird game early and have that tattooed on your soul's resume for the rest of eternity.

3. Look at the cards a little closer, closer, until you see right through them to your own hand.

Now, there's a hand you can do something with.
Hank

♦ ♦ ♦

At the first part of his email, I laughed 'til I cried. Then I cried some more just for the hell of it. I had to remind myself why Hank and I had decided to be just friends. What a great guy, and a great friend.

Then I reread the last part, about the hand I was dealt. I knew I had somehow lost myself in the relationship with Kurt. That I had spent so long trying to make it work, to find somehow to make him happy, assuming that it must somehow be my fault if he wasn't happy. Just wait a damn minute, Laura. He was responsible for his own happiness, wasn't he?

I had long since forgotten what I wanted, who I was. I had been living in a chapter of Kurt's life, and not living my own life. I was going to have to be very careful about that. I did not want ever again to be a chapter in someone else's life. (Unless it was Hugh Jackman's life…)

I wonder how many of us make that mistake? The accommodating, nurturing people so often do. The nurturer carries on willy-nilly, not even realizing what he is doing. But, is he responsible? Aren't we all responsible for holding on to ourselves? Oops, I just wrote "he" twice. That should be "she."Right, then: The hand I was dealt was not bad. I just needed to play it.

Chapter 9

Crazy 'Till Proven Otherwise

"If you could kick the person in the pants responsible for most of your trouble, you wouldn't sit for a month."
~ Theodore Roosevelt

And now, for one of the weirdest stories from my online dating years. This one completely decimated any lingering Warrior Woman status.

It was Halloween night. Do you think that should have been my first clue?

The most ridiculous experience of all, in those years of online dating, has to be Jerry, from Vermont. Oh my. I have put off sharing this story with you, afraid that you will think I am the biggest idiot, the biggest fool, on the planet. Ah well, so be it...

My excuse, and I'm sticking to it, is that it was in my first few months of online dating. I didn't know the ropes, was naive and trusting, thought people were who they say they were. Ahem.

Biggest lessons learned? Meet for coffee first. Or, if there is a long distance between you, meet halfway. And in that case only for lunch, not for dinner. Always. No exceptions. Period. Please, I beg you.

Jerry lived, indeed, a long way off, up in Vermont. But he had found me (my filters were for only 50 miles). And once he had written, he intrigued me.

He was a molecular biologist, had completed a fellowship at an Ivy League college, then worked in research for many years. Very smart guy. But he got tired of it due to the big business aspect of the research world. Disillusioned, he left that field completely and became a financial advisor for a well-known firm. (Before we met, I even called the financial firm to confirm he worked there. I was proud I was covering the bases.)

He had uploaded half a dozen good pictures and he looked to be very much my type: tall, slender, dark hair, fit, handsome, well dressed. His profile was well thought out and well written. He lived in a log home he had designed himself, and then built overlooking a mountain in Vermont. The fact that he loved classical music, especially Bach, Mozart, and the entire Baroque realm was a plus for me, as was the fact that he loved gardening, spirituality, philosophy...

My, oh my, I was hopeful! He was intelligent, self-deprecating, and sounded caring and truly interested in finding a partner in life.

We had two long conversations on the phone, where I confirmed that we seemed to have a great deal in common, and yes, he did make me laugh. What was not to like about this guy?

Francesca warned me not to get my hopes up and repeated her adage: "There is something wrong with all of them."

Hank's warning was: "Vermont? Be careful of Vermont. It's where a lot of weird people go." (This seemed a very harsh generalization at the time, and my sincere apologies go out to all you normal nice folks who happen to live in Vermont…)

Since my practice was fairly new in Connecticut, I assumed I could move more easily than most people and start again in a new place. May as well start again building a practice in a new town, I thought. Or state, even.

(But, how on earth could you spend enough time together to ascertain if the relationship was going to work? How do you *date* from that distance? But that's another conversation).

Jerry invited me up, convincing me we needed more time together than just a lunch or dinner, and that I could stay in a hotel or at his house. After talking it through, in the end it did seem to make the most sense for me to go up there, instead of him coming down to me. In retrospect, I wondered why I didn't insist he drive down to my neck of the woods on a Saturday morning, planning to go back on Sunday. He could stay at a hotel if it felt like we wanted to spend more time together. Anyway, silly me, I agreed to drive two and a half hours up to Hartford, VT.

I know, I know, I'm an idiot.

When Jerry tried to convince me to stay at his house, he confirmed that he had two spare bedrooms and would honor any boundaries I set. I politely declined. So, I am not a *complete* buffoon. I checked out a couple of local hotels and found they did have rooms available. I didn't care how nice he was, or how well our first meeting went, there was no way on earth I was going to stay at his house.

In spite of Hank and Francesca's warnings, I felt hopeful. I might have found an interesting and attractive partner! One with potential attraction and lots of commonality! And moving to Vermont would be fine with me; I had always loved driving through and visiting that beautiful state.

I drove up late on that Saturday afternoon, which was, I repeat, Halloween. I was planning to meet him at a restaurant in his town. I was so hopeful, I didn't even mind the gazillion dollars I spent on gas. Sixty-five of them, to tell the truth. The expense and effort seemed, at the time, to be a worthwhile investment. "Speculate to accumulate," or something like that.

Did it work out well? What do you think?

First point: When he walked into the little restaurant, I had to hold my jaw shut. It wanted to fall down. He looked *nothing* at all like the photos he'd posted, which must have been at least fifteen years old.

Second, he had a tooth missing. I will repeat that and must even break the all-caps rule: HE HAD A TOOTH MISSING. A front one. Seriously. I kid you not, and I would never dare to make this up, because you wouldn't believe it. I didn't.

Thirdly, he wore hiked up jeans, three inches too short, with paint spattered on them. So, old pair of painting jeans and work boots? To meet a woman for dinner? Insulting, to say the least.

Was this a *joke*? Had he taken a bet with some friends?

Then, to make matters worse, he hauled out his wallet before we ordered... He counted his money. In front of me. Why? He said he had to make sure he had enough cash. Couldn't he have thought about that before I got there, driving two and a half hours to meet him? He didn't have a credit card he could plop down so I didn't feel embarrassed watching him see if he had enough cash? This guy was in the financial advice field, for God's sake. I wondered at the time if he was hoping I would offer to help out. That's what it felt like. With that thought came this one close on its heels: "Over my dead and maggot-ridden body, Pal."

Truth is, I ate as fast as I could, fully intending to high tail it. I choked down a bit of pitiful Caesar Salad, made with wilted iceberg lettuce, greasy, tasteless salad dressing, and overcooked, dried up chicken bits. From a little diner restaurant. The fork by my plate was encrusted with someone else's food and I had to ask the waitress for a clean one.

He invited me back to the house, and I had to clamp down on a plethora of retorts that wanted to spring forth.

Instead, I simply declared firmly, "no," to that idea. He looked completely taken aback and asked for an explanation. I could have hauled off and let him have it right there in the parking lot, but was concerned for my own safety. As it was, I expressed tiredness, and told him I was heading home. I made sure there were other people walking to their cars before I said this. Witnesses. Then I hopped in my trusty CRV and headed south, without so much as a backward glance.

Steam began to escape from my ears. I got angrier and angrier as I drove the same damned two and a half hours home again. In fact, I was beyond livid. At him for his deception, his use of non-current pictures, his tackiness, his tasteless lack of consideration. But, mostly at myself, for driving all that way, with all that effort and expense.

I vowed **never again**. At the time we were organizing our get-together, I was not very comfortable with the fact he didn't offer straight away to drive down to meet me, but I gave him the benefit of the doubt, easy, helpful soul that I am.

I arrived home mortified, exhausted, disappointed, hungry, poorer. And painfully wiser.

I never lived it down with Hank. He called it the most expensive Caesar Salad in the world.

I decided that from then on, they were all crazy until proven otherwise.

Chapter 10

Online Dating as a Way of Life and Loquacious Larry

"Never mistake a clear view for a short distance."
~ Paul Saffo

Staring at the computer...

To hell with dating sites. To hell with men. To hell with you, Computer. I felt like hurling the laptop out the window. There was a large pond at the entrance of the townhouse complex, and I could just reach it if I threw real hard. A laptop acts a bit like a Frisbee, I bet. It would be fun to find out.

I have a theory about this. Someday, maybe 200 years from now, they'll be draining that pond for some reason, and they'll dredge out 894 various laptops, iPods, phones, Tom-Toms, and all the rest. Half of them will be mine.

But I had to keep trying. Being alone the rest of my life was just not an option for me. But as for the whole online thing, this was getting ridiculous. Pretty soon, I'd have to look in New Jersey and New York, having worked my way through all the guys in Connecticut.

My thoughts were a tangled mess. Do I have the courage to try again? Are all guys on dating sites self-absorbed, suffering from giant-ego syndrome, or lying scumbags? And if do find someone again, will it ever last? Or is it hopeless?

You must know the percentages aren't good for people who have been married before. That the second marriage is no more likely to last than the first. Almost like, hey, I got divorced, it wasn't that bad, I can do it again (get divorced, that is.) We now dispatch our partners with a constancy and speed unparalleled in American history. Or, anywhere else in the world for that matter. I read somewhere that seven years is now the most common length of a marriage, so there might be a jar of pickles in the fridge I've roomed with longer. I remember a birthday party I went to where a woman told me her 20-year-old cat had died two weeks before, and she was devastated. "Lived with him longer than my husband," she said to me.

Let's forget about the odds of whether another marriage will work or not, let's revisit those odds of even finding someone you would feel at home with. Someone whose sentences you find yourself finishing. Someone whose breath makes you weak in the knees, because it smells like newly-baked bread. Someone who *gets* you. You and all your weird ways. Like the fact that you startle easily? Like when your partner/husband enters the room behind you and speaks to you and you jump two feet in the air and look, for all intents and purposes, as if you've had a seizure. So, he needs to learn to call out a little "Helloooo" before he comes in so you don't die of a stroke. (Kurt used to get irritated, and say, "Jeez, Laura, I *live* here... ").

Can you find someone willing to do that, go through that, to get you? I guess we never know what the odds are but we keep trying, we keep looking. I sure do. Being alone is highly, highly, *highly* overrated (repetition intended).

I must now address this "being alone" thing. I am truly damned sick and tired of hearing we should be OK alone. Or more than OK alone. We should be just *great* by ourselves. We should love ourselves and be happy on our own before we can truly be with someone else. Blah blah, freakin' blah. What a load of manure. I actually saw the following sentence, these very words, on a self-improvement website, which I will not identity (I'm sure there is a plethora of sites pronouncing the same rubbish, anyway.) "If you aren't happy single, you won't be happy in a relationship." What a complete crock.

The psychobabble of the last thirty years declares if we aren't happy alone, then we have poor self-worth. Seriously? I know people who have excellent self-worth who are not happy alone. We are a lonely society: thousands or millions of single people, living alone in little boxes, in apartments or houses, worrying that they are not happy alone. But, they pretend they are, so people will not judge their self-worth. I repeat, seriously?

So here is the point: Man, as a species, is not *meant* to be alone. We are directly descended from primates who gather, live, and thrive in families, and are rarely, if ever, alone. And, for those who would argue we have evolved since our chimp days, I beg to differ. We have not changed much at all. In fact, it seems to me we may have grown in mental intelligence, speech, and logic much faster than we have evolved away from our basic instinctual driving forces, such as fear of predation, protection of our own, hoarding of foodstuffs in the line of that protection, and competitiveness to be Alpha – best, strongest, and fastest.

OK, sorry, I got carried away.

Where was I? Ah, looking online... I always hear people complain that the internet-dating world is full of weirdoes, liars, players, and jerks. Sure, I did meet a few men that met those descriptions. There was one extreme case of a lying player named Rick – you will meet the scumbag a bit later. And I encountered one or two severe cases of narcissist personality disorder. (You know the kind, the guy that talks endless about himself and then stops and says, "But, enough about me. What do you think of me?").

However, even though it is true that I met some of these strange, damaged, sad people, my experience tells me there are no more of them online than there are in the rest of our society. The percentage is probably about the same.

OK, on second thought, maybe a wee bit higher because so many balanced, healthy people are already in long-term relationships and plan to stay there. That skews the odds somewhat. You know the old line, "all the good ones are already taken." I hoped not. All I needed was one.

The one, hopefully.

The next guy I am going to tell you about was **not** the one. We didn't even make it to the cup-of-coffee date. There are many of these, of course, that don't make it to the email stage, or to the phone stage, or to the coffee stage.

But, this guy is actually memorable: Loquacious Larry. Yes, that's my name for him. Larry was, indeed, his first name. I added the title, and it fit him like a wetsuit. Snug and very revealing.

He reminded me so much of my mother. When she gets on the phone, she talks non-stop, from topic to topic, wandering around, like a sort of mild verbal diarrhea. I murmur, "uh-huh" and "oh, that's interesting" and "really?" from time to time to get through it. My sister, Katie, says the way to deal with it is always to allot 45 minutes, never less, because you can't get off the phone anyway. So why fight it?

In my case, I always picked up my latest *Fine Gardening* magazine, poured a wee glass of Zaya rum or my favorite port, "Six Grapes," and settled in to pass the time as best as I could.

My mother is one of those people who can talk for a full ten minutes about a doughnut she bought "the day before yesterday, Tuesday... Or, no, wait a minute, was it Wednesday? No, that's right, it was Tuesday because I thought it might rain. No actually, I think it was Wednesday because they changed the oil in my car..." She doesn't trail off long enough for you to interject, but carries right on. Anyway, this doughnut was "cream-filled, actually it was a kind of a Bavarian cream, or was it called vanilla cream, no, wait, maybe it was."

And on and on. You find yourself wanting to shriek, "I don't care, Mom, I don't care about the damn doughnut!" My mother can talk the hind legs off a zebra and then you feel your brain curl up and crack like a very old tennis ball in the desert. OK, that's mixing metaphors, but you get it.

My friend David explained it by saying she is terrified of silence. She just has to fill it. With anything. She will read road signs aloud if you are unfortunate enough to have her as a passenger in a car. She reads street signs, ads, anything, so there won't be a silence.

Once when I lived in Santa Monica, California, and she had come to visit, we were driving to Trader Joe's, only about 20 minutes from my house. I hadn't actually noticed before that many of the street signs were named after states, but I found this out in an interesting fashion. My mother, when conversation wore thin for a nanosecond, began to read them as we drove by. She read "Arizona Street"… Then a pause while we drove the next block… "New Mexico Avenue"…. Utah Street"… Then a very brief silence, which she promptly filled with, "Are these streets named after states?"

"No, Mom, the states were named after these streets."

The sarcasm was totally lost on her.

She replied, "Really?"

In any event, I realized there were 47 more of them and contemplating that made me want to hurl myself from the car onto the road. Being run over by the next vehicle somehow seemed eminently preferable to being trapped in a car with my mother for any more minutes. Or states. At least lying in the hospital bed it would be quiet.

Larry was so like my mother, on the phone. When I called, I caught him driving home from work. He told me he would be in the car for about 40 minutes, so it was a good time to chat. And chat he did. He talked non-stop for the entire time, about his life, his daughter, his son, his divorce, his property with the apple tree that absolutely must come down due to its mystery illness, his brothers, and their jobs, and wives and kids, and dogs. I even learned all about his cousin's trouble with his wife adopting a pit bull. I learned all about his youngest son's troubles at school with possible dyslexia. I learned all about his ex-wife's irrational dealing with their 12-year-old daughter. And on and on and on. And on some more.

He didn't even learn my last name. Or, that I lived in Fairfield. Not because I was so unwilling to give out any personal information, but because he asked exactly nothing. In actual fact, I don't think he drew breath for the entire time we were on the phone, or I would have jumped in with some reason to get off. I had no chance. I nearly went to the door to ring the doorbell, so I had an excuse to hang up.

But, oddly, after while, it became rather interesting to see how long he could go without asking me anything. I even considered going to make a cup of tea, come back in ten minutes and see if he had even noticed I was gone.

At the 40-minute mark, when he arrived home, he said he had to go as his son Jesse had just arrived with his ex-wife and he needed to spend some time with him. OK. Fine. Bye.

I got an email from him late that night telling me how very much he enjoyed talking with me. Talking *with* me? Also, how nice it was to get to know me a bit. *Know* me a bit? When did that happen? Did I blink and miss it?

Chapter 11

Those Pesky Expectations

"Expectation is the mother of all frustration."
~ Antonio Banderas

I was in a frenzy. I had arranged with Kurt for him to pick up the rest of his stuff, the stuff Francesca thought should still be burning and smoking in a pile of carbon on the lawn, out front, as he drove up.

It had been eight months– why did the thought of seeing him send me into a frenzy? The divorce proceedings were marching on, relentlessly, and the unpleasantness, the harshness of all that should have been enough to cut the strings to Kurt. To end the connection. How could I not be over this guy?

I dropped by Hank's photography studio – I'd never been there and he wanted to show me around. He'd only recently found this space and it had taken some time to get it all working just the way he wanted it to. It was a huge loft, with wonderful natural light and gorgeous light oak wood floors.

He had all the highest tech equipment in the way of lights, filters, green screens, and photographic gear. What a wonderful place to work. There were bistros and diners all around, and fun little coffee places.

After the tour, I plopped the bottle of Cockburn's Ruby Port down on the counter near his computer, and he searched around for a couple of clean glasses.

"What are you up to this weekend?" he asked.

Oh, dear, I knew I had to 'fess up.

"Kurt is coming up."

"What?!"

"Wait, hold on. It is just to get his stuff. There's a closet full of clothes and other things that belongs to him. With winter here, he needs his heavy sweaters and coats..."

Hank grimaced.

"It's a good thing," I assured him. Firmly. "Closure."

"OK..." he said very slowly. He studied my face.

"Am I crazy to let him come up?" I was hoping my voice and face were not consumed by desperation.

"Yes. You are crazy. But, that's not the point. Maybe you will break the habit that is Kurt. Remember the Old Sanskrit proverb: "The last moments of an ancient pattern stink the most."

I grinned.

Hank continued. "Will it help you in some way to see him, maybe realize he is a turd, or ugly, or a fat slug, and you don't really love or miss him?"

I hesitated.

"Oh," he said, a small triumphant smile formed on his lips. "You think you can win him back. You are already planning what to wear to look hot and gorgeous and win the bugger back."

"No, I'm not! How could you think that?"

He waited, watching me steadily.

"Honestly!" I said confidently.

He waited some more.

Then I sighed. "Well, hell, Hank...."

"Yes?"

Just well hell, Hank.

We sipped our port for a bit in silence. I tried to hold back tears. And some embarrassment. It is hard being seen and known and understood, when you are, in truth, just attempting to shine yourself.

"And..." I spoke hesitantly. "He might even stay the night."

As Hank started to sputter, I hurried on. "Maryland is so far to trek back and forth in the same day! And it seems unkind to make him stay in a hotel."

Hank stared at me. I think he was speechless.

"I know. I'm completely nuts." I muttered.

He nodded. "Hang on a minute, Warrior Woman. Kurt's visit can be hell or heaven, or simply neutral. It's not the actual man that brings the rain; he means well. It's the construct of 'What we expect' that always sets us up for the gut punch. Kurt doesn't actually own a dung bazooka, nor would he fire one at your lovely torso if he did."

Dung bazooka. Perfect.

Driving home, it struck me again, the "expectations" piece of the whole thing. Francesca had mentioned it. Now

Hank was laying it out for me in a picturesque fashion. That concept sure was taking a large chunk of the pie lately.

The next morning, when I stumbled to my computer after tea and toast, there was an email for me from Hank. He had thought about it further.

Hank to Laura:
Here's a mental experiment:

Scenario 1. Suppose you're starving out in the middle of nowhere, and you come across a fine peanut butter and jelly sandwich on a paper plate. You'd love it, and it would taste great.

Scenario 2. Suppose a friend tells you about an amazing restaurant, which has the best food on earth, amazing decor and clientele to die for, and a two-month wait for the reservation. The night finally arrives, you're starving, and they place before you the exact same fine peanut butter and jelly sandwich.

Which one disappoints, and why?

In Scenario 2, your brain screams out: "This is not what I expected!"

In Scenario 1, your brain goes, "Yum."

In this case, the 'friend' that tells you all about the restaurant, is our culture, with all its glory-stories of love and Hollywood endings that smell of roses. (Whereas, most actual "ends" in Hollywood probably smell about the same as your average trucker's behind).

Either way, the reality is: It's a nutritious sandwich.

Maybe we should let our stomachs run the show.

Love Hank

♦ ♦ ♦

Friday evening started out rough, with Kurt due to arrive the next day. As I sorted through clothes and other paraphernalia in the closets and drawers in order to pack up everything that belonged to him, I tried hard not to indulge in sentimental, self-wounding moments. I tried not to "feed the pain-body," as Eckhart Tolle called it.

So, I popped an old dance CD in the player that I had created years previously, with my favorite rock and upbeat music on it: Mellencamp's "Hurts so Good," Seeger's "Old Time Rock and Roll," some great Santana, and "Fooled Around and Fell in Love." There was even a bit of 70s disco by the BeeGees, and Abba's "Dancing Queen"... I was dancing around and singing and feeling good! It was working! Look at me! I was over him!

Yay me!

Then I found it. The loose-weave green sweater I'd given him on our first Christmas together. It looked, felt, smelled just like Kurt. I was thrown back to the last time he had worn that sweater. It was on that perfect spring evening when we had dinner on the patio outside of the Four Seasons in New York City. It was one of those magical cool evenings: perfect temperature, perfect food, perfect wine, perfect vacation, perfect marriage. I thought.

Isn't smell just the most evocative, powerful sense? The smell of mustard throws me immediately back to hot dog roasting over campfires when I was a kid. The smell of cloves sends me right back to Mike, my first boyfriend in high school, who brought me a peach-colored carnation each time he came to pick me up. Oh my.

The smell of a man's pipe always reminds me of our elderly neighbor, when I was about seven years old. His name was Mr. Wright. But, I was absolutely convinced he had told me his name was Mr. Good. In fact, I was convinced of it, and even argued with my mother about it. I called the dear grandfatherly soul Mr. Good for years and years, until my mother managed to straighten me out. But, Mr. Wright was way too kind to complain, and later told me he loved that I called him "Mr. Good."

Back to our sense of smell, and the infamous green sweater. This bitter January evening, I couldn't help myself, and all the upbeat dance music in the world could not compete with the smell of Kurt. I buried my nose in the soft folds and breathed his soul into mine. Or I tried. All I breathed in was pain – a dagger that took my breath away. Months later and the smell of the man rendered me incapacitated.

After many tissues and a good nose-blowing, plus some acetaminophen for the headache I had given myself, I dug out my shoebox full of scraps of writings. I've always written my story or poem ideas down on a small notepad I keep in my handbag, and when that isn't available, on anything that comes to hand: restaurant receipts, napkins, or a bit of an old envelope. Toilet paper, if necessary. Even something funny someone says, I scribble it down and wonder if I will tuck it into a poem someday. In the meantime, all of these ideas get crammed, willy-nilly, into the shoebox, in the closet. Once in a while, I look through it, and transfer the ideas that snooze through time and transcribe them to the computer. Good ideas might just be in there, for that great poem or novel I plan to write someday.

I found the musing essay on love I had written a few years earlier. In fact, I wrote it before I met Kurt. I thought he was the answer to this description. He was not.

Love Beyond Choice

It is surely a mystery. Love transforms us. Researchers, authors, poets, and philosophers have all tried to pin down the elusive ingredient. What makes one person so precious to us? Is it pheromones, is it hormones, is it neurotransmitters? Is it the energy of the heart itself that recognizes a long-lost mate?

There are stages or depths of love. There is the rapturous, addictive phase of attraction – that "in love" feeling that may last a year or two. But sooner or later, the moment arrives when you choose that person, even when faults, flaws, and weaknesses surface. You choose him, and that is the moment when you commit.

But, beyond these stages, deeper than these, there is something more. There is a more powerful, soul-connecting kind of love. I am talking about the kind of love that can walk you through fire or deserts, or convince you that you can dig a swimming pool with a spoon for your beloved. A love that can survive heartbreak

tragedy, trauma, age, and infirmity. The love you see between two old souls walking slowly through the park on a Sunday, holding hands. Through illness, through tragedy, or through despair, the light burns on in the heart.
This is the source of strength unparalleled. It can build mountains and ride the deepest waves with endless fortitude and determination. It is fed by tenderness and understanding. It is fed by compassion and kindness. It is fed by time and the pursuit of dreams. It seems a force stronger than death itself.

It is a love beyond choice.

That is what I wanted, those seven years before. Now, I'd settle for some peace in my heart.

Chapter 12

"See ya..."

"A man is a poor creature compared to a woman."
Honore de Balzac

As it happened, Kurt's weekend run to get his stuff was completely anti-climactic. He was with me for less than an hour.

In actual fact, he was not with me at all. He just raced in, the tension and anxiety flowing off him in palpable waves.

It was as if he had become autistic since I had seen him last. He could not meet my eyes. He told me he was heading straight back, no explanation. He piled the stuff into his car and headed off, with a quick hard hug and a "See ya..."

See ya? The livid burning lava that swelled in me kept me from the pain I would have otherwise experienced. See ya? After seven years together, marrying, buying a home, moving up here to Connecticut, coping with his narcissistic kids' meltdowns, and wading through all the other ups and downs of life... together.

Well, I guess that's all it was worth. See ya.

As the anger wore down (I just can't hold anger for long – it makes me feel so terrible), it crossed my mind that I had believed I'd forgiven him. Completely. Maybe I still had more to do in that area. Forgiveness. Hmmmm. What a concept. Don Henley said it so well: "I think it's about forgiveness, even if, even if, you don't love me anymore."

Kurt felt so bad. He must have apologized for hurting me about a zillion times and had signed up for 37 years of therapy. (I suspected he had done this just so he could honestly tell me he had and it would make him feel less guilty.)

We had, in truth, been duct-taped together for a long time. And the tape was now finally wearing thin. Why on earth was it still there at all? When it finally tore free, maybe I would be able to move beyond the hurt and the memories and the loss and the rejection and the abandonment. More time, that's what I needed. More time to get used to being without him.

Back to forgiveness. That would do it. Wouldn't it?

First, let me explain to you that Kurt is a childlike boy-man. Now, I figure I am smarter, more advanced than some in our species. Please take my word for it – although I do confess and admit the evidence for this statement is also wearing thin, as I write my tale of woe.

Anyway, you'd think I could keep a childlike boy-man interested, especially if you agree, in the karmic progression of things, that human beings are men first. Maybe we come down here from wherever it is we live as spirits, and return as a man, over and over again until we get that right. We learn to "do" man, very well.

Then you come back as a woman. Which, face it, is a lot tougher. Women go deeper, value truth more highly, connect more deeply with friends and family, and tend to more greatly honor and value that truth. And, their lives are much harder: more pain, more stress. They are the queen-pin of the family, holding it together.

Maybe when you've had plenty of lives as a man, you reach a place of being able to handle intimacy and truth, and have achieved some distance along the spiritual path. Then you come back as the simplest, stupidest woman.

I told one of the "gentlemen" I met for coffee of this theory. His blunt retort was, "Hell, I want to stay a man. I'd have to start off as some slag-assed bitch in a trailer park for a few lives, so no thanks."

"Charming," I said.

Do I need to tell you I did not have a second date with this person?

Let's look deeper. Maybe it's true, maybe we are more advanced on the consciousness path than men are. Then why do we so often display less self-worth, less confidence? Because we feel less of a sense of entitlement? We certainly suffer more. Maybe we start off with healthy self-worth and over time, it gets beaten the hell out of us.

As I pondered this theory, it slowly came to me that I could be wrong. The older I get, the more recurrent is this thought. In fact, I find myself finishing plenty of sentences with, "But I could be wrong."

What if, in fact, it works the other way around? It is true we women have a head start with the degree of intuition we experience, and are more in touch with our emotions. So, perhaps it's actually *easier* for us to get on the consciousness path. To evolve, to grow. Perhaps we are programmed to do so.

Maybe we are women first, on the evolutionary ladder, as we do this work more easily. Then we go on to lives as men, and can hardly remember having done the work as women. So, it takes us forever, if we get there at all, to get in touch with ourselves and wake up.

Where does Kurt fit in all this? His downfall was that he was haunted by his own demise. Years before, he had taken the first wee steps toward self-improvement, by reading, mostly. That was the first curious, seeking part. The easy part. Part of my initial attraction to him involved our endless talks about consciousness, spirituality, evolution of the human species. Why we do the things we do. Why and how things work in the universe. I love all that. Even knowing I will never have the answers, I can talk about it, ruminate on it, endlessly.

However, he couldn't walk the walk. He didn't live a very conscious life. Living a conscious life involves telling the truth, living your purpose, taking conscious control of your decisions, practicing kindness, and committing to truth, courage, and honor. He blew all of those. You have heard about the big things, how he lied to me. That is hardly living a conscious life.

But, add to that so many little things. Just one example: he left every light in the house on, all the time, so when he went back in a room it would already be lit. When questioned about it he retorted, "I can afford it, to hell with it. I've earned the right to have all the lights on."

Seriously? It is not about that, to anyone trying to tread more lightly on our planet. It's about doing the right thing for the sake of doing the right thing.

Perhaps it is better never to jump on the path in the first place, call it what you will: self-improvement, personal growth, consciousness... Because once you do, you can't go back. It's as if you've opened a door, you can see the opportunities, you have seen a light or a vision. The world does not look the same ever again. You will not be able to turn a blind eye to Monsanto's greed. Mindless hours of "The Apprentice" or the Kardashians will never have the same appeal. Neither will cheating on your husband. Or lying to a colleague. Being unkind or rude to someone begins to come with a nasty price. Your own self-judgment. Sounds tiring? Sometimes... but I realize I wouldn't want it any other way.

Kurt was aware of the path, but lacked the courage to walk it. And cowardice is its own punishment.

The phone rang, interrupting my contemplations. It was Francesca. Bless her, she knew Kurt was due that morning.

"What's happening, sweetie? Is he still there?"

"No. He was here a minute and a half. Grabbed his stuff and said, "See ya.""

"See ya?"

"Yup. Nice, huh? Not even, "See *you.*" But "See ya." Anyway, I don't want to talk about it. Maybe I am best off forgetting the whole thing. I am clearly not entirely over Kurt, and I can't seem to find a man who is not insane, a liar, or just mildly moronic... So maybe I better just be alone."

"Well you have had your share of weirdoes across the table for coffee haven't you? But you'll find someone, eventually, if you keep looking. But you know, honey, I'm just not sure, anymore, about the whole thing."

"You mean dating online?"

"Or dating at all. Maybe even worse than that... Being with a man at all. They just take so damn much looking after. Don't you think?"

"I guess," I muttered.

She plowed on, her voice strong and sure. Seemed she had been thinking about this. "I just don't want to look after a man anymore. It seems like to them, what we're doing is somehow not as important as what they're doing."

"But where does that come from? I mean, seriously?"

"We do it to ourselves, we women, don't you think?" she asked. "The Baby Boom generation was supposed to change all that, and I guess they made some strides, but honestly, we're still doing it. It's down to the Millenials. I hope they change it. But, I grew up in the 'Be quiet, your dad is tired from work' syndrome. Did your mom say that?"

I sighed. "Absolutely. Daddy relaxed with his feet up watching ancient episodes of some Star Trek spin off, while Mom and Katie and I cleaned up the kitchen, as quietly as possible. Of course, Mom worked all day as a bookkeeper for a local dentist, then went to Stop and Shop, then made dinner, while she put the laundry in the dryer. Then she cleaned up afterwards, and we helped."

Francesca said, "Yes, exactly.

How much of that is changed? Men cry, "That's not fair, we help!" But, do men help around the house? Put those words into Google and see what you get. I did. A large study was done of 17,000 men and women in 27 countries, and sure enough, married men do less housework than women. They are much more important than we are, remember? Ha ha.

Furthermore, marriage seems to make it worse. The researchers pointed out that married men contributed significantly less housework than those men who were living with their partner/significant other, and were not married.

Maybe marriage, in itself, is an institution where we tend to comply with or mimic what we learned when we were children. It somehow brings out the traditional in all of us. Even those of us who consider ourselves "out of the box" seem to tuck back into the damned box when we get married. Then there was the fun study I saw that showed that men who did housework had "more and better sex" than those who didn't. Awesome! I should have taken a copy of that report to any serious date I might have had.

I found yet another study that concretely showed Men Don't Do Dishes. (We knew that...) It panned out that men did about a third of the total housework and women about three quarters of it. Men in Sweden, Norway, and Finland did the most.

That does it. I am moving to Sweden.

I couldn't agree with Francesca's assessment that men were more trouble than they were worth. She had had her 25 years of wonderful team partnership, with her wonderful William. I had yet to find it.

I couldn't give up.

Chapter 13

I Know What I Want

"Attitude is a little thing that makes a big difference."
~ Winston Churchill

Oh my, so many coffee dates. I had met so many men that I was disillusioned, even feeling hopeless. There must be someone, somewhere, I thought, with whom I could have a nice partnership, some fun, someone who liked some of the same things and we could at least make good roommates?

Can you believe I am saying this? Does the word "romance" or "chemistry" or "magic" figure anywhere at all in that scenario? Sadly, I was past thinking those things could apply anymore.

Here is another strange tale from these dating days: the aborted meeting I had with a weird, sad, depressed, bitter man.

He seemed rather interesting in his profile, an attractive high school teacher and coach. Tall, in great shape, a boyish smile, and on the phone, I discovered some humor and an easy, natural intelligence. Sounded good. After the normal preliminaries, at which I was truly becoming an old hand, by now, we arranged to meet at a Starbucks.

I got there first and found a table. He arrived soon after, and I recognized him easily. Good news, I thought, he actually looks like his picture. Maybe a little older than his photo, but this is pretty standard. And shorter. Also standard. (Men lie about their job and their height. Women lie about their age and their weight. Yup. Almost without exception).

He looked around the room, then got in the coffee/tea line. Oh, on second thought, maybe that isn't him? He hasn't acknowledged me, and I know I look like my pictures.

He was in line for a good five minutes, while I sat there, wondering if I should get up and join him, as he clearly could not have seen me. However, it was a busy Saturday and I didn't want to lose the table.

He got to the counter, ordered his latte, waited a few minutes for it, picked it up, sprinkled some cinnamon on top, and wandered over to me. He plopped his drink down across from me, straddled the chair, and said, "You must be Laura."

I immediately thought (and had to stop myself from saying it aloud), "And you must be a jerk." What kind of a jackass invites a woman for coffee, then buys his own and doesn't wait to see if she wants one? He never even asked. I sat there, wondering what I should do.

He started to talk, telling me right out of the gate I was the 137th woman he had met since he had signed on to online dating sites. I trust I will be excused for the fact I couldn't think of much to say to this. "How nice" seemed rather inappropriate. But, I saw why he didn't buy a coffee for each one. At $4.00 a pop that would have been $548.00.

Just to see how rude he could be, I said, "Maybe I'll get a coffee." He didn't respond, just leaned back in the chair and looked around, obviously preparing to kill some time while I did just that.

I didn't bother to get a coffee. Or, stay to talk to him. I just got up and walked out. He wrote me an email asking what had happened, and I didn't waste the time to reply.

The funniest part? A year later, Mr. Jackass wrote me an email on Match saying he liked my profile and pictures and would love the chance to get to know me. I sent a short email pointing out the obvious (to me) fact that we had met once before and didn't like each other. He had the nerve to write back saying, "Let's try again, maybe it will work this time."

I actually laughed out loud. Yes, sometimes the whole process is very, very funny.

♦ ♦ ♦

One evening in the middle of the week, I logged on. 14 new emails. 18 winks. A wink on most of these sites is a quick way to say, "Hi" when you are in a hurry, a bit shy, or a bit lazy. If the guy you've winked at takes a look at your profile and is interested, you will get an email in return. I rarely send a wink, as I think it just speaks more to the level of interest you have in someone if you take the time to read his profile, and write a line or two that is specific.

To make online dating work best for you, you do need to sculpt and edit and re-sculpt and re-edit your profile. Then do it again. Dare to write about your perfect dream-partner, right there, in your dating profile. Ask for exactly what you want! Why not? May as well get it on the table.

What I want in a partner:

▶ Attraction. Yup. Can't do without it. Don't even want to try.

▶ Someone with the same values in life, a similar sense of spirituality and close to me in political views.

▶ A great sense of humor, the same sense of humor as I have! And someone who values highly the power of laughter in his life.

▶ Someone who believes in the pie-plate theory. I'll explain. This is someone who wants to be part of a team and for that team to be a pie-plate on which all other pieces of our life-pie rest. The pie-plate holds up, or supports, all the rest of the pieces of our lives together: work, house, garden, children, each side's family commitments, goals and dreams, daily preferences. Everything sits on the pie-plate and is held up by it. This kind of partnership was even more important to me because I had no children. To me, my husband was, and would be again, my family.

However, not many men, I believe, can willingly serve on the team by combining with their partner to make a strong pie-plate. I sure have had plenty of blank stares of incomprehension when I have tried to explain this to men I am dating.

▶ Someone who is not afraid of intimacy, who understands intimacy, gets that this is where truth and a profound relationship exist and thrive.

OK, I must address this intimacy thing for a minute... So powerful, so connecting, such heaven inherent. Why do women get this so much more easily than men? So few men get it at all. They run from it, hide, or deflect to something else the moment they encounter it! So many men do not even value truth in a relationship. They don't know that the truth of intimate connection *is* the relationship, so their marriage is defined by the degree to which they understand and revere it.

I wanted a man who believed in: "...a fearlessness, an unashamed insistence on intimacy," as Tom Junod of Esquire magazine put it so nicely.

I'll never forget the therapist I was seeing who told me that 80% of his private practice was women. He said all his colleagues, as well, mostly work with women. Not because the vast majority of screwed up human beings are women, but because they are the ones who aren't afraid to admit they are flawed, and they seek help. Then they are not afraid to work on themselves. And, on their relationship. He went on to explain that the vast majority of those women were seeking help because they had no intimacy or connection or truth in their relationship. That made them depressed. Here was his moral ambiguity: to give them antidepressants so they could better handle being in a lousy relationship? Or, to suggest they insist on intimacy, connection and truth in their relationship, or leave it? Knowing this may result in them being on their own again? Because he acknowledged that out there in the world, there are few men who are willing to share that intimate place with a woman.

Face it, it is a bit hard to filter for intimacy on an online dating site! However, if you know that intimacy is what you want, what you need, you can carefully put a feeler or two out into the air around the coffee table when you first meet, or at the first lunch and see how well he responds to intimate conversation. You just might get an indication whether he's up for the challenge or just looking for the door!

Bottom line of this online dating thing:

I appreciated online dating because I could wade through potential life mates, or just hot dates, by knowing exactly what I was looking for, filtering like mad, and then going for it.

Doesn't sound romantic, I hear you say? Think of it this way: is it less romantic to spend your life alone, going to work every day, wondering how to meet someone, showing up at increasingly bizarre singles events, or being set up by your friends with all their strange single acquaintances?

Just as a momentary aside: have you ever wondered about how well your friends know you? A good way to find out is to accept a blind date with someone a friend or acquaintance wants you to meet. Someone they think is "absolutely perfect" for you. You end up spending a shockingly bizarre evening with someone completely out of touch with anything you like or are interested in. You have no sense of humor in common. Your values are different. Perhaps he is a rabid materialist and you are into spiritual endeavors. He lives on the golf course in his spare time and you love gardening so much that you have your mulch guy on speed dial. Maybe he wants to travel, to see everything, in retirement. But you may have spent too many long hours on airplanes, and visualize a homey retirement, where you don't have to pack and stand in lines and get on buses in the sky.

When you drive home, you think, "Wow, Jack and Jen have absolutely no idea who I am." This can make you wonder.

Online dating eliminates all this. You can set up parameters and criteria that are essential to you.

On the other hand, if you just want a little foray into a big sexy hunk for a weekend, that works too!

I guess you need to know what it is you truly want. Here is an important piece I had not considered carefully until Hank brought it to my attention. He once asked me the following question, and he asked me to think about it seriously. We were munching on pizza at my place, fire crackling, bottle of Merlot disappearing. He asked, "If you could have three months with the total love affair of your life, complete passion, perfect love and adoration, true bliss and happiness, and then be hit by a bus and die… OR live the next thirty years peacefully with a good friend with whom you have no passion, which would it be?"

It didn't take me even one second to deliberate. "The first scenario, of course. Not one shadow of a doubt. The first one."

We stared at each other. I turned it over to him. "And you?"

"Oh, the friend, and living thirty years."

Yikes. And here I was thinking I knew Hank pretty well. We'd been good buddies and "cry-on-each-other's-shoulders friends" for several years, by this time. I just couldn't believe he wouldn't go for the passion. To feel that alive? To feel that bliss and rapture? Wouldn't that be worth dying for? Perhaps Jane Austen would be shocked, and caution me to lean more towards sense than sensibility.

Either way, this conversation with Hank reminded me of something I heard, somewhere: An unfulfilled woman needs many "things," but a truly fulfilled woman, in love, could sleep on a board. The truth is, I'm looking for a man to share my board.

*"I still believe in love. I always will.
It's my blessing and my burden."*
~ Walter Kim

Chapter 14

Analyze This

"Sometimes I wonder if men and women really suit each other. Perhaps they should live next door and just visit now and then."
~ Katharine Hepburn

The next wee tale I want to share with you (wee being the operative word), begins with my responding to an attractive professorial looking gentleman, who showed a wonderful command of language, and an aptitude for philosophical thought. We talked for hours on the phone, about my breakup, and how I needed to work on "stuff" unprocessed about my relationship with my father. (This was probably true.) He was in his element, as he was a psychotherapist, with a successful practice in Hartford.

I thought, at the time, that this showed a great generosity of spirit, in offering his valuable time to discuss my possible issues. Hmmm. A tiny skeptical voice inside me whispered that he was just showing off. Showing me how very much he knew and how wise he was. I hushed that voice, telling Inner

Laura to get over herself, to give this man the benefit of the doubt, to be grateful for his profound insights.

We decided to meet. And not for a psychotherapy session (phew), but at Chili's in Fairfield. Brave, huh? Straight to lunch, rather than the usual cup of java.

I have always been wary of trying to have a relationship with people in this profession. Many of them seem to be a little damaged, neurotic, and drawn to psychology, perhaps to help themselves. Some do get help, and then can truly help others. But, many of them want to process everything all the time. That's the word. *Process.* They want to stay in the dark stuff, work on it, figure it out, feel it again, process the hell out of it. And, they want to sign you up for months and months. Of course. This is how they get Mr. Psychotherapist, Junior into braces and through college.

My friend and colleague, Karen, and I have talked long about this. She dated a psychotherapist for a year, and told me adamantly that, in retrospect, it was actually 364 days too long. He analyzed her, noted everything she did and what that might mean, commented on which buttons of hers were pushed, how, speculated as to why, then hypothesized from which parent that button derived. And, they talked about **process,** until she wanted to ram his process into a small dark hidden place.

I have never dated a therapist, so I was open-minded in this instance, because the man was 51 years old and had been working in the field for 25 years – surely he would have worked out most of his "stuff" in his "process?"

The very least I expected from such a professional, in such a profession, was honesty. His profile said he was 5'9," and the picture, taken from slightly beneath him, as he sat in a dark green leather chair at his desk, made him look big, bear-like, even. I was drawn in. I thought Mr. Psychotherapist-man had potential.

As I arrived at the restaurant for lunch, I was nervous, once again fixing my hair, and checking in the mirror that I had no lipstick on my teeth or anything descending from a nostril. A few deep breaths, Laura, and remember, no one looks like their photo. I re-reminded myself of Francesca's idea, for the 342nd time, "There is something wrong with all of them." *All of them.*

I chuckled, drew in a deep breath to settle my little attack of nerves, and strode purposefully towards the building.

There was a little, no, tiny man waiting by the front door. But of course, that couldn't be him. This guy was **short**, I mean 5'2". He was dressed all in black: black shirt, black western jacket, black jeans, and black cowboy boots. Then I looked at his face. He took off his sunglasses and grinned. Oh my God, this was him. This tiny little man. Oh, I know I am showing myself to once again be small (pun intended) but he was literally four inches shorter than I am and I was in flats that day. I'd have towered over him if I had worn the dark red ankle-boots with the high heels that I'd almost chosen.

"Hey, beautiful lady!"

He gave me the once over, (gazing up at me) while I stood with a stupid, fixed smile on my face. Anything to mask my shock – dismay, even.

"You are even more beautiful in person!"

I babbled some drivel that I hoped was appropriate. I have no idea, now, what I might have said.

Over lunch, he confessed that he was so thrilled to meet me and to find that I wasn't old, fat, or ugly. That I hadn't lied on my profile. He said so. In so many words. I couldn't believe it when he launched into a diatribe about the many women he'd met who had lied on their profiles, put pictures up that didn't represent them at all, or were years out of date.

But, there he was, in all his tiny glory.

One of my weaknesses: I like tall. I like big. My father was tiny and I have always gravitated to the opposite, to a tall strapping man. Shallow? Maybe, but I know what I like. Chemical attraction does figure in, even if we try to pretend attraction will grow in time (it doesn't.)

And remember, here, folks, there is an inherent *honesty* issue at play. It isn't that I have anything against short guys, but he lied to get me to meet him. Now I feel for him, for I realize that being that short must make it very difficult for him to find a partner, or it certainly would limit a man. I guess he hoped that the very force of his personality would win me over so that the height thing wouldn't matter.

In fact, I learned quite a bit about his personality that day. His nature included a gigantic ego that could poke a mighty hole in the ozone layer.

In retrospect, I sort of wish I had called him on his deception. I mean, *called him on it*. Let him have it with both barrels.

Nope, I chose kindness. (Or do I give myself way too much credit when, in truth, I copped out through a startling lack of courage?) I was polite and survived lunch, just listening to him talk about himself and his wonderful career.

Then, I couldn't get away fast enough.

Though, for a brief second, the evil little me, inside, was tempted to reach right out and pat him on the head as I left.

I emailed him that I did not want to take "this" any further, and in his reply, expressed great shock. He professed to being stunned, after such great conversations and such a "connecting and sharing" lunch.

Really? Next.

If at first you don't succeed, try, try again.
Then quit. There's no point in being a damn fool about it.
~ W. C. Fields

Chapter 15

Aftermath: The time in between

"Were it only that some enchantment would step in for us all, to change what we have into what we wish for. To bridge the awkward gap between all of our many befores and afters. Because, for every after found, a before must be lost."

~ Lotty, "Enchanted April"
Stageplay by Matthew Barber,
Adapted from the novel
by Elizabeth von Arnim

Hank was over for the evening. And, oh my, such a state he was in. He had broken up with his on-again, off-again girlfriend, Fiona. He loved her desperately (how can that be a good thing... to love desperately?) and had tried again with her. She got angry about something (read, "scared of committing and getting hurt") and had left him *again*. Yet he kept trying. About five times.

So maybe being stupid about love is not just a female thing. Sorry, Hank.

As I puttered around the kitchen, serving us dinner and opening wine, Hank fiddled with the crackling fire, adding logs, and poking them around. We'd decided to eat in front of the fire, so I brought the first tray in: Hot bread, wine, glasses, cutlery, etc.

When I came into the living room with plates, I noticed he was once again checking his phone for messages. This was about the tenth time since he'd arrived, half an hour before.

Pusskin had given up on my sitting down any time soon, so she was all up in Hank's face, wanting some affection and pets. He put his phone down (good for her!) and gave her a stroke as she curled up on his lap.

Hank mused and voiced his thoughts. "OK, Kitty, *now* you want attention. Last time I was here, you gave me the great walloping cold shoulder. Hmmm. You know, women are like cats... leave their hair everywhere... they are a little cuddly with long stretches of aloof. They play when *they* want to play... Picky eaters."

As I handed him the wine, Hank finally seemed to see me for the first time that evening.

"I'm self-absorbed here, sorry, Laura. You seem sort of down, too, is something up?"

Well, I may as well tell him, I thought. Misery loves company and all that.

"Well, the week started out dreary and then tanked. You know about Kurt's Flash-Visit up here to get his stuff..."

Hank nodded and grimaced.

I carried on, "Well, that was fun. **Not**. And, today I found out that I have to move my practice. The clinic owners filing for bankruptcy. Lost their shirts in the 2008 debacle... And people are just not going to massage therapists, naturopaths and acupuncturists like they were before the recession hit."

"Oh, hell, Laura, that sucks."

"Yeah, it does. I have a couple of months, which is a good thing, but finding the right place to practice takes some serious thought... and time."

I didn't have to tell him that my heart wasn't in it. Being abandoned and navigating the subsequent divorce was enough of a load, I thought; tackling this additional life-change was an added weight.

I returned, again, to the kitchen to serve the stew in wide Italian pasta bowls. You know the ones, they have big olives or fruit painted on them, and just manage to make food taste better, somehow. I handed him one, along with a plate of hot crusty garlic bread. Then, I plopped myself down into my big soft red leather chair, and sipped my wine, leaving my stew to cool for a while.

Hank said, "Well, maybe we should shop for coffins now – you know, while we are still alive... "

That got my attention. "Excuse me? Oh. Ha. Ha." I said. Then I saw his face. Was he serious?

"Hank...."

"What, is that not done?" he inquired innocently.

'You rat." I muttered.

"Gotcha. Ha ha. I just wanted to get a lid made for it, of beveled glass... I could use it as a coffee table. Why not buy it now, rather than when you're dead, when you don't even get to see it?"

I chuckled.

Hank lifted a big spoonful of steaming chicken "stoup" to his mouth, and I watched the bliss on his face. No, that's not a typo: Stoup. I made a homemade chicken stew, which was more like a soup. Or, a chicken soup that is thick so it's more like a stew. He had named it Chicken Stoup. It consists of reduced chicken stock, so it has strong flavor, and I add onions, mushrooms, potatoes, and a dash of red wine, seasonings, and whatever vegetables I have around. Big chunks of carrots, and sometimes Brussels sprouts, or even parsnips. It is never exactly the same twice.

Hank was such fun to cook for. As he chewed, he moaned softly and uttered an appreciative yet emphatic, "Oh. My. God."

I said, "Well, I don't know about shopping for coffins, but the other day my accountant asked me if I had a will in place, and it got me thinking... I don't even have anyone to leave my little bit of money to – what's left after the stock crash nailed it. That made me even more depressed."

Hank muttered around a mouthful of stew. "I know. I was trying to work this morning, trying to keep busy and not think about Fiona. I keep reminding myself of Tolle's mantra in about not feeding the pain-body. It works for awhile, but not for long."

"Yeah," I replied. "Or what about his wonderful piece of advice, 'Stay in the moment.' What if this moment *sucks?*"

Hank grinned. "And as for the Warrior Woman, has she buggered off and left you to your own devices?"

I nodded. "Pretty much."

We ate in silence for a few moments. I wanted to share with him that I ached for the loss of the dream, for the loss of how good it was with Kurt, how comforting. I wanted to 'fess up to intense loneliness, to a sense of being completely uninspired to ever attempt it again.

No. Don't do it, Laura. Damn well stop feeling sorry for yourself. Hank is down and you need to cheer him up. So far, you've been no use at all with that. Talking about coffins and wills... Honestly, woman.

"But," I said, in an attempt to focus on the bright side, on positivity, "things will improve. They have to, right?"

Hank wiped his mouth with his napkin. "I read once in a physics book, that if the universe was even 1% predisposed to favor the Good over the Bad, then given the great course of time, the world by now would be a dream-like paradise."

I nodded, wondering where he was going with this.

He continued, "That tiny amount of favoritism, extended over millions of years, would have led to a huge amount of difference by now. So, the author concluded that the universe was absolutely neutral, caring neither for one nor the other. Boy, that bummed me out."

"Yeah," I muttered, nodding. "Evidence for atheism, I guess."

"Yeah, but in the next book I read, the author said that the universe was in such an unbelievably delicate state of balance, it's a total miracle that it hasn't fallen out of balance and blown itself apart, yet."

"Ok...." I said slowly.

"He concluded that something unseen, or someone, was controlling that delicate state of balance."

"Oh, that sounds better. Let's go with that." I pushed my bowl aside and reached for my wine glass.

Hank clinked my glass in a toast, then said, "But maybe it's as simple as this: A man goes to a psychic for a clue as to the rest of his life. The psychic tells him not to worry, that a few years from now, there will be lots of money. Endless money. She tells him that he will touch many people, so many people. He spiritually prepares himself as best he can, not knowing any other details. Two years later, he gets a job with the New York Transit Authority, collecting tolls on the Triboro Bridge."

Oh, how I laughed! You never knew what this guy was going to say next, and I did so enjoy his company. And he made me think.

Later that night, long after Hank had headed home, I found myself pondering the whole thing. I jotted him an email.

Laura to Hank:

I've been thinking about your notion of balance of the universe, or our little dumb corner of it... What if entropy, its sole job being to break everything down, in its indisputable fashion, is only combated by the power of life-force energy? All of mankind keeping some sort of fragile order? We're not doing too well, huh?

♦ ♦ ♦

Hank to Laura:

I think you're right. But, don't knock the importance of human beings. We've extended our mind power out into nearly every sphere of science and philosophy, and into music and art... So perhaps our brilliance is somehow involved in this balancing act.

♦ ♦ ♦

Laura to Hank:

Maybe just 'wanting,' is what drives the whole forward momentum. Maybe we're an engine of some kind, fueled by desire. If we ever got what we wanted, then we'd stop 'desiring' and the whole entropy-deal would spin out of whack again. Who knows?

Anyway, back to the mundane.

*I think I finally may be turning a corner where Kurt is concerned. I must – I **must** – move on, think forward, like you keep telling me. Be open to the new, the hopeful, the possibilities.*

But get a load of this: Kurt called after you left last night and hesitantly suggested that we try it again. I guess his therapy is going well and he's decided he may have messed up where I'm concerned. Gee, whiz, ya think so?

*But that whole idea sounds **completely** stupid to me. I think I would have to be too stupid to live if I went for that.*

So, I am going to turn this corner and keep it turned. No peeking back around the corner for one last look. Don't you think that is the hard part? The desire to look back.

♦ ♦ ♦

Hank to Laura:

It's the whole being alone thing, isn't it? Being alone for now might be hugely scary. However, most of that thought is an illusion. We're born, breathe, live, love, dream, die, all of us... definitely alone.

Alone= being far enough away from the next guy so you can't hear him fart.

Alone= saying something so stupid you're mortified, but luckily no one hears you.

Alone= having time to listen to your own thoughts.

So.... for now, we're alone...

A postcard arrives from your soul: "When you're finished crying, come follow me, there's one hell of a view I want you to see with me."

Love, Hank

♦ ♦ ♦

"Your pain is the breaking of the shell that enclosed your understanding."
~ Kahlil Gibran

Chapter 16

Bag of mixed nuts

"Every strike brings me closer to the next home run."
~ Babe Ruth

    I didn't give up. I still longed to meet someone, and I lowered my expectations again and again, in order to achieve it. By this time, my expectations pretty much resided in the dark damp basement... along with most of my hope.

    I was disillusioned, oh, about 437 times, but then I'd endure another long, lonely weekend, and creep back to the computer, log on, see some winks or emails, and hope would peek its little elfin head up and smile at me, tempting me. So, yes, there are many more stories, most of them short and sweet, thankfully, of strange men I met, almost met, or wish I hadn't met, in my five-year online dating extravaganza.

♦ ♦ ♦

    There was a guy, can't even remember his name now, who went on and on about looking forward to meeting me.

For some reason I decided, with this man, to talk by email a few times, as I didn't see an enormous amount in common, and thought this would be the best course. (Was I wising up?)

I finally called him and chatted for a few minutes, and he was very nice. He pushed again (politely) for a meeting. So, we organized a coffee meeting for the next day. I went through the usual preparation, nerves, preening, etc, and then proceeded to sit there, and sit there, and sit there, in the coffee shop.

He didn't show up. I assumed something went terribly wrong with his car, or his dog died, or there was an emergency with one of his kids, but I never found out. After an hour, I gave up. He never emailed to apologize (he didn't have a phone number for me, for which I'm glad, in retrospect.) Nothing. I'll never know. I worried a little that he had been hit by a truck.

However, I saw his activity level online, which read: "Active in the last 24 hours." I checked every day for several days. He was not incapacitated in a hospital bed. I was so annoyed, I could have put him in a hospital bed myself.

Now, now, Laura.

I will never know what changed his mind.

♦ ♦ ♦

This next scenario happened more than once. It involved a very dishy hunk who approached me in a friendly email, flirting wildly. He told me I was gorgeous. Told me he loved Alison Kraus, bluegrass and country. He expressed his fascination with alternative medicine.

I opened up his profile and saw several pictures of a handsome man who looked remarkably young. Oh. He was 26. I nearly asked him what he was going to be when he grew up...

I answered his long email with a nice thank you, I am flattered, etc. etc., but told him I had no desire to be Mrs. Robinson.

His reply read, "Who is Mrs. Robinson?"

I shot back, "Uh, you know, *The Graduate*? With Dustin Hoffman? Classic movie from the 60s or 70s?"

He must have been online at that moment, because, quick as a flash, he came back with, "Oh, right... Ok, I'll ask my grandmother about it."

Since I couldn't think of a polite reply that did not involve the F word, I didn't reply at all.

But, I did wish I could send him a coupon from Dairy Queen for an ice cream cone.

♦ ♦ ♦

Then, there is the guitar player/singer I had high hopes for. He was attractive, lived fairly close to me, was interested in poems and song lyrics, and loved the same music: soft country, folk/rock, folk/pop, bluegrass. He was warm and approachable and we had a nice conversation on the phone.

When we finally met for lunch, we had a pleasant enough time. That's the best I can say. There was zero attraction for me. It's that simple. I said nothing at the time, having learned the hard way not to tell the person then and there, "I am not interested," or "There is no attraction." I had one very livid man send me the worst email *ever* after I did this. He tore me off and called me every kind of heartless, insensitive, impolite, thoughtless... You get the idea.

Therefore, no, I did not say anything. I wrote him a nice email when I got home.

The email I got in return was steeped in self-righteousness. "Well, I don't know what you could possibly be looking for? We have everything in common and there was not a moment's silence. It seemed perfect to me."

He just didn't get it. Some people are so self-absorbed that if they are attracted then the other person just has to be as well.

◆ ◆ ◆

Then, there was the sailing dude from the Mystic area in Connecticut. He guided tourists around in his boat, was fixing up his 18th century house near the beach, and sounded wise, thoughtful, and spiritual in his profile.

But, oh, my, what a condescending, arrogant, know-it-all! On the phone, after a few minutes of pleasantries and warm-up, he sailed off into a professorial diatribe, telling me how much he could teach me about spirituality. There was his way and the wrong way, and everyone but him was an idiot. I wanted to gather up all his bullying blarney and shove it sideways down his throat.

When he asked if we could meet, I politely said I didn't feel we had enough in common to meet. Oh my, I can't even tell you the things he said in reply to that. He was unkind, cutting, dismissive, and offensive. Suffice it to say he ended with, "Well, what a waste of my time. You turned out to be a cold, hard, bitch."

Oh, my, how very spiritual of him! I was reminded of the Hara Krishna guy at college who came up to me to tell me God loved me. I told him I was not interested in his spiel and was late to class. As I hurried away, he shouted after me, "Well, then fuck you, bitch."

Hmmm. Nice.

Believing you are on the path of consciousness doesn't make it so. I think this is a common enough state of affairs. I have met so many New-Age-flaky-crystal people who have read all the books about spirituality, but can't rise above their own ego. The more they read and study and meditate, it seems the more condescending they become, some of them anyway, thinking they know it all, are better than you, are further along the path.

I'll never forget one particularly irritating Course in Miracles meeting I attended years ago in a Unitarian church on a Saturday afternoon. About 25 people sat in a big circle, the session being led by a dude who was a pompous pain in the ass. I am displaying restraint in this assessment. He spoke slowly, all his words dripping with a sort of forced kindness, authority and command. Can you say fake baloney crap? At one point, he responded to one person's query with, "Perhaps you are not yet ready to understand this piece, my friend. Everyone is at a different place on the path, and you may not be there yet."

At which point I stood up, gathered up my stuff and marched out. I wanted to tell him *he* was not there yet. That he simply didn't get it *at all.* Instead, I just strode out, fuming, knowing that if I had spoken up, I would find it hard to stop once I got started. I knew, anyway, that it was hopeless; he would have just acted as if I was not ready for his crap. He would have said I didn't get it *yet*.

I ranted and griped to myself all the way home. A real pet peeve of mine, this is.

The truth is (in my opinion, and as always, I could be wrong) as soon as you think you are further along the path, you aren't.

♦ ♦ ♦

Oh, and I simply must address the guy every woman encounters at least once: the married guy. Who says he is single. Or that he is newly divorced, or waiting for a divorce, or that he is separated. Some lie or other. And you discover through some unfortunate means, that he is not. Not any of those things. He is, in fact, still completely married.

My story of the married dude goes like this. Carl was a great guy: divorced (according to his profile), attractive, and we had plenty of common interests. We had coffee together, then lunch, then dinner. Things were looking very good.

Then he invited me to his company annual "do" which included a dance... ooh, a live band and a chance to dress up! I met him at the event, held in the banquet room of a large hotel/conference center, about a twenty-minute drive for me. It was half way between my home and Carl's.

I wore a gorgeous black and white knit (read form-fitting) low-cut slinky dress, with a skirt full enough to swirl when I twirled. Oh my. Figure in sheer black stockings, high black and silver heels, and all silver jewelry to set off the black of the dress.

I felt great.

Round linen-covered tables filled the banquet hall, and each was festooned with flowers and candles. And ample bottles of wine and champagne! There were eight people per table, and all of them seemed to know Carl. I would go so far as to say there were many friends of his there. Welcoming to me, they clearly liked, admired, and supported Carl, taking turns telling me how great he was. I heard from them how excited Carl was to have met me, how it was time he was happy. Delighted for us both, they declared, that we had found each other, and wished us the best! I was touched and impressed that he had such good friends.

He rose further in my estimation.

We had such fun, and oh, how I danced!

A little before midnight, as the band was beginning its wind down, and playing the Foreigner tune, "I Want to Know What Love Is," an older gentlemen strode toward us on the dance floor, and asked to cut in. Carl graciously conceded, introducing me to his boss, who I will call Harry. I saw a moment of vague disquiet on Carl's face, but simply put it down to the discomfort people often feel around their boss. Harry paid me a lovely compliment or two, saying he had been wondering who the "lovely lady" was that Carl was dancing with. I told him we had met on Match, but had only been out a few times.

"Carl's a good guy." Harry smiled. "Everyone likes him here. But I wasn't aware that his wife had given him a divorce."

I was silent, my legs still danced in time to the music, in spite of the thundering in my ears.

Harry continued. "And to have found such a beautiful and charming woman so quickly – well I hope it works out – I am happy for you both!"

I excused myself and dashed to the ladies room, where I splashed some water on my face, and took a few minutes to compose myself. I thought about just high-tailing it to my car, and heading for home.

But I returned to the table. Carl gave me a big hug.

"I missed you!" he exclaimed. "You were gone so long!"

The rest of the story is obvious. I asked him, right then and there, if he was divorced and he had the grace to flush bright red, then the color drained away and left him pale. He followed me to the parking lot, full of excuses: "My marriage is over, has been for a long time... We lead separate lives... " Blah blah blah.

I let him have it in the parking lot. What I hollered, word for word, is not repeatable here.

'Nuff said.

How to protect yourself from a liar like that?

I have no idea. Every woman I have ever known has lived some variation of this experience.

♦ ♦ ♦

Here is a quick one: the guy who sounded like a cross between Daffy Duck and Elmer Fudd. He had seemed very interesting in long emails before we ever talked. When he called, and I first heard that voice, I thought he was playing, just fooling around. I almost laughed. Just in time, I realized he was serious and did not know he sounded like a cartoon character.

Now while I regret that I might have been passing over a very nice guy, I confess I just couldn't get past it.

♦ ♦ ♦

There was also one man I can only identify as Dr. Jekyll and Mr. Hyde. He made me want to hide, that's for sure. (Sorry.)

This is yet another weird story. The man was an Emergency Room physician at Saint Francis Hospital in Hartford, and seemed to be an intelligent, warm person with a great sense of humor. Our vibrant and amusing first coffee meeting after a promising phone call and emails led me to think there might be something there.

He asked me to dinner, and he drove all the way to my town, where we met at a lovely bistro. I dolled myself up in copper colored slacks and jacket, lovely vibrant scarf, and dangly earring. I was looking forward to it!

Then over our shared bowl of mussels in white wine and cream, he told me his story. Oh. My. God. The *Story*.

There were two ex-wives, one he married when he was 18, as she was pregnant. The second tried to kill him. I didn't find out why, exactly, just the fact that he gained a broken jaw in a physical fight with her. This ex was currently in prison.

I looked around for the reality show cameras that were surely pointed at me.

He was not through. I heard about his "Hogs" (motorcycles) and told me, rather proudly, it seemed to me, of the various accidents he'd had with them. There were long detailed descriptions of how long he had spent in the hospital as they repaired this leg, that arm, this collarbone.

He shared with me that me he was a member of AA, both for alcohol and drugs, and was desperately trying to remain sober.

"Oh, congratulations. How long has it been?" I did want to encourage him.

"38 days, so far," he replied. "But I have high hopes that this time I will be able to hold steady. Of course, there is still the drug thing – cocaine is my favorite."

He must have seen my face.

"Oh, don't worry," he said quickly, "it's not heroin, or anything."

I couldn't come up with a remotely intelligent reply to this. "Oh, that's good," I think I must have said. Or something like that.

Oh, I almost forgot, there was the bankruptcy. He launched into the fact that his Chapter 13 legal status was half over and he'd be able to start building credit again. In two years time.

Now I know I need to be open, tolerant, helpful to my fellow man... To give people the benefit of the doubt.

But, not this much. Any one of that list of hard-core life events would have given me pause. But, all of them?

Furthermore, was all this confession shared with a kind of sadness, embarrassment, or determination that seemed real? No, the only way I can describe it is that he seemed proud of being the bad boy, the black sheep, the dangerous guy.

He was *so* not the man for me. I was so not the woman for him, either.

Was there not one balanced, healthy man out there in the world?

> *"But if you do not find an intelligent companion,*
> *a wise and well-behaved person going the same way as*
> *yourself, then go on your way alone,*
> *like a king abandoning a conquered kingdom,*
> *or like a great elephant in the deep forest."*
> ~ The Buddha

So, that is what I was left with. Maybe I'd have to be an elephant.

Chapter 17

To Game or Not to Game

"Trust me honey, men don't appreciate that women give willingly. A thousand years of evolution later, it's still about the chase."
~ Lisa Gardner, *Touch and Go*

One Saturday morning in June, Francesca helped me move all my files and client paraphernalia to my new clinic space. It was in Shelton, a few miles north of where I lived in Fairfield, but not a bad drive at all.

I had found a wonderful clinic that needed a naturopath to round off its alternative medical staff, in an environment that suited me. This was a stately old house built at the turn of the twentieth century, which had been renovated to hold professional offices. It offered that warm, inviting feeling of honey-colored wood floors and beautifully carved newel posts. Paneled walls graced some of the main floor rooms, and there were curio cupboards and deep windowsills in the bay windows, where Tradescantia, and spider plants flourished. The house even had heavy pocket doors – oh, I love a gorgeous pocket door.

My office was at the back, on the main floor. In trip after trip, we hauled boxes of files and my essential books. All morning we worked, until we'd organized it enough to be ready for me to start on that Monday. By early afternoon, we stopped to relax.

My new office opened onto a patio with wrought iron table and chairs tucked amidst big pots of begonias, pink and purple Impatiens, deep blue Lobelia, and tumbling trailing Vinca. I had brought humus and a salad, plus a celebratory bottle of champagne. Although it had lost most of its chill, we popped that sucker open.

That Saturday in June felt balmy and sweet after the long, snowy Connecticut winter. The newly planted flowers all around us filled my heart with deep pleasure as they always did. I filled my patio at the townhouse so full of containers of annual flowers you could hardly move around them.

I sighed. "Thanks for your help, honey. This would have taken forever without you."

I handed Francesca a glass of bubbly, if tepid, champagne. She waved away my thanks and clinked my glass in a small toast.

"To you, Laura. You've found a great place to practice. Now, here's to your finding love, real love."

"Oh, I couldn't love again. Not the way I loved Kurt. Not possible."

We munched in silence for a few minutes, hungry after our morning's exertions. Then, I scrunched up my paper napkin and tossed it down on the table. "I just feel so unsure of myself. After all that therapy, years ago, I should be the healthiest person alive. Can't you buy psychological health?"

Francesca grinned. "It's something to do with choosing happiness and contentment, and finding a way to stay there, no matter what nonsense or chaos is going on in your life."

I nodded. "Yeah. There is a great line from *Eat, Pray, Love* – you read it?"

She shook her head.

"Oh, it's awesome, I'll lend it to you. It's by Elizabeth Gilbert. Anyway, she said she suffered from, get this, A '*heartbreaking inability to sustain contentment.*' Isn't that just a horrifying concept?"

"Never being satisfied? Uh, yeah... "

"I know when I was younger," I said, "I always thought happiness was waiting for me with the next job, or achievement..." It didn't occur to me when I was twenty-five that I could just be happy. Be sitting there doing nothing, that that was OK.

We all, in our culture, just push so hard all the time for happiness. I have always wondered about the whole "Life, liberty and the pursuit of happiness" idea. Isn't that basically flawed as an aspiration? I mean, is it healthy to be chasing the next success or item or acknowledgement that we think will make us happy? Should we, in fact, be trying to *pursue* happiness?

Or, wait, is that a *good* thing? Is chasing goals and dreams an offshoot of the passion of life? If we didn't, would we be just a crowd of sleepy lemmings?

Maybe, in fact, truth is somewhere in between. Maybe we need to push, to pursue a passion, in order to achieve something. That is how all the great pieces of progress have happened, across history. But then stop, rest. If we are constantly pursuing, then we are not seeing the happiness inherent in just being in the moment. After all, isn't that what all the teachers of spirituality are saying? Isn't happiness there if we just let ourselves *be*?

Perhaps if we slow down, happiness will catch up to us.

Francesca was speaking, but I was off somewhere in this little thought-wheel. "Sorry, honey, what?"

"I was saying about that line – "hard to sustain contentment." Don't you think men find it harder to sustain contentment than we do?"

"Perhaps," I replied, wondering where she was going with this.

"Well, listen to this eye-opener from the other night. I was having dinner with Keith and two friends, political acquaintances. Mary Lou and her husband were trying to talk him into running for Connecticut State Senate, and Keith invited me along as his potential wife, I guess." She grinned.

"But you aren't sure about that," I offered.

"No, not at all," she said more adamantly than I expected. "Not sure about ever marrying again. But anyway, here's the point. I thought it would be a stiff, rather boring evening, all political talk, but I ended up in a wonderful conversation with Mary Lou. She's from Georgia, and I think some women from the south have a different take on relationships than we do – perhaps a different upbringing from those of us north of the Mason-Dixon line."

I nodded. "Yes, it does seem like it."

"She has a completely different take on the whole thing. She firmly believes the sexes are opponents. She is about our age, maybe a little older – 55-ish? So, a holdover from the older days?

"I haven't spent any time in the south," I said, "but I do think there are some older mores in place there, even still."

Francesca nodded, shrugged. "Maybe not a generalization we can make, but listen to this. Mary Lou described the game of dating, catching your mate, marrying him, and being the power behind the successful man. Get what you want without him knowing you are getting what you want. Make him think everything great is his idea."

"Holy moly, seriously?" I was a bit shocked. "Sounds like 100 years ago!"

She nodded again. "She said, basically, keep him off balance, so he stays interested. This was her mainstay: be mysterious, don't give it all, make him work at it, keep him wondering, keep him off-guard... She told me, very quietly, that I needed to get Keith married, right quick, before the passion wore down."

My mouth opened and closed a few times but no words came out. I threw my hands up in the air. "I got nothin'."

Francesca laughed as she nodded. "I know!"

My whole life I have balked, completely, at the notion of games between the sexes. Haven't we outgrown that crap? I gave up playing games when I was 14. What a ton of work. Plus, it is so fake, so planned, so dishonest. So much for *intimacy,* right?

I had always given myself wholeheartedly to relationships, been eager to please, been as sweet as I could be. So far in this lifetime, it wasn't working out well. So, should I have played games, hidden my love, been less nice, to keep my boyfriend/husband interested? My skin crawled at the notion. If Mary Lou was right, this is the only way to keep them interested. Well, that's truly, completely, undeniably awful.

However, here is a wee bit of hard evidence that may back up her theory, although it pains me greatly to point it out. A few nights later, I was on the phone with Francesca, and she told me she was still thinking about all Mary Lou had said.

"I've had enough." Francesca muttered.

"OK..." I said slowly. "About what?"

"I've been stupid. I've been completely available to him over the last few weeks. I knew he was particularly stressed with work, with family stuff, and I didn't want to add to his hectic life... I mean, I love him – I want to *ease* his life."

"I know, babe," I said. "We want to be easy-going and flexible. Sounds good to me. To be helpful, thoughtful... "

"But... and here it is," she said. "He'd started taking advantage of me. So, I decided to put my foot down, hard. No more Ms. Nice Guy... "

I heard her lighter clicking, and she drew in the first breath from her cigarette. I waited.

Francesca said, "A couple weeks ago – I don't think I told you about this – there was another New York conference involving his firm, and he called to wheedle me into driving into the city with him. He said he'd be busy at the conference on Friday, and then we'd stay for the weekend just to have fun."

"Yeah, but you've done it before, right? You have a great time – hasn't it been worth it?"

"Perhaps," she said slowly. "But why doesn't he give me some notice? He must know about these conferences in advance – they are planned weeks ahead! As it is, if I want to go, I have to change my plans at the last minute. And sometimes I think he just expects me to."

I nodded, realized that she couldn't see that on the phone and said, "Right. Typical."

"Well, that night, Mary Lou's words rang in my ears. I explained to him, in no uncertain terms, but very sweetly and with great regret, that I was busy with auditions for Community Theater the very next Monday evening. I told him that, sadly, I simply could not drop my preparations to go into New York for the weekend."

There was a pause. I asked, "So? What happened?"

"Damn it all, if he wasn't suddenly more attentive. Seriously! Remember I told you he'd sent me flowers recently? That was a day or two after that call. *And,* he's been more loving, more considerate, and has begun to treat me with the respect I want. That I deserve, damn it! As if maybe, just maybe, I have a life of my own to consider."

"What a novel concept!" I said.

"I guess it comes down to the fact that you teach people how to treat you," she said. "I was teaching him how to treat me."

Ouch, I thought to myself. Was that really how it was?

Francesca said, "You need to remember this, honey. You are so good... Maybe you are too good. Maybe you need to develop a selfish gene."

I didn't know what to think. Later that evening, after Francesca and I had hung up, it hit me again. Selfish gene? I had spent my adult life trying to reduce selfishness. To be more self*less*.

Surely, there was someone for me, a partner somewhere I could be myself with? Someone I could love and cherish wholeheartedly without holding back?

But, this I will concede: When I studied creative writing in college, I learned a basic rule: in fiction, be it a story, or book, or screenplay, one needs tension or conflict. This, hopefully, resolves to an ending that is balanced and harmonious. You need conflict, or you have no story, no plot. If you just watched Cinderella's story from her wedding day until a year or two later when they had a big old bust up, you'd be bored to tears!

We love conflict. We want to see how our heroes will face challenges and hurdles, and then feel the relief when they resolve it. Happy ever after. (Not really, but stay with me here for a minute...)

Maybe it's the same with relationships. Maybe something too even, too calm, too pleasant, is not exciting enough. You wonder why so many women seem to be drawn to men who are a little dark, a little dangerous, a little difficult. Like Heathcliff, from *Wuthering Heights*. Or, Ross from *Poldark*. They can't be pinned down, or there is a sharp edge to them, somewhere. Within healthy limitations, maybe we like *tension*. A bit, anyway.

Here's an example that may support this theory. During this five-year-dating-hoo-ha that turned out to involve 88 guys for a cup of coffee, I met a wonderful man named Tom.

As he was also a naturopath, we had buckets in common, spoke the same language, and were very comfortable and peaceful with each other. We were just so in tune. However, there was no tension. We both acknowledged that it was potentially the best match we had ever found. But, does the perfect match, on paper, excite or stimulate us? Or, if we are too similar, do we miss that magnetic attraction of the different, of the opposite?

The bottom line was: I didn't want to play games. I just wanted to take my ball and go home.

But, on the other hand, it kept coming back to this: I wanted to find love. It felt as if I were on a seesaw.

Later that evening on the phone with Hank, I told him I was once again renewed in my determination to find someone to love. Wholeheartedly. Not hold something back.

I sighed. "Maybe it's just around the corner. I have another guy to meet Friday night."

"Oh, great, babe! I knew the celibacy wouldn't last!"

"Hey," I protested, "I am not going to *bed* with him, this is *coffee*."

"Yeah, right. It's been more than a year, when are you going to give up coffee and get laid, honey?"

Good question.

Chapter 18

Barry Big Bear

"One half of the world cannot understand the pleasures of the other."
~ Jane Austen

It was not to be, the next Friday night. Getting laid, that is. And it was not destined to become that great wholehearted love, either.

I just had one single coffee date with a huge bear of a guy, named Barry, from northwestern Connecticut, up near Kent or Washington. Somewhere up there. His profile pictures revealed an attractive man, with a wonderful, friendly smile. He had light blond hair, like a big Viking, or as I decided, once I met him, a big, blond, Kodiak bear. He collected antiques and had just bought an old house he was working on. This sounded interesting, and then I was won over completely by the deep sexy voice on the phone. Men with deep baritone voices, who make you think of those great voice-over actors, have always done it for me.

Although I did not immediately find a great long list of common interests with Barry, I decided to move ahead anyway. Just to play devil's advocate, how many times have you met someone and you're just fascinated by them, validating the old "opposites attract" thing? Maybe it isn't for us to say that someone will or will not be interesting to us. There are so many people I find fascinating who don't share the same interests as I do.

I need to be a little adventurous, I thought to myself. Maybe I will meet someone interesting who will expand my horizons. If you only consider meeting people who line up perfectly with all your loves and interests – the same spiritual inclinations, interest in alternative medicine, psychology, philosophy, love of Thai food and loathing of Mexican food – doesn't it seem a bit like answering an ad for a used piano?

After a short, but pleasant, phone call, I agreed to a coffee date. I drove up to Newtown to meet him, a good halfway point. By this time, I was starting to realize I should have bought shares in Starbucks.

I was early, he was little late, and I sat there nervously, fussing with the clip in my hair, trying to be cool, wondering if the sexy, designer jeans I was wearing made my butt look big. Helpful, deep, intelligent thoughts like that.

As he walked in the door, I saw that he looked just like his picture – on occasion, this does happen! Great big smile and he was so huge, his head brushed the top of the doorframe and light couldn't squeeze around him. He was an eclipse. Not fat. Solid.

He was wearing a flannel shirt and old jeans, and one of those puffy, padded, vest thingies that always reminds me of a life jacket (remember *Back to the Future* where Marty was asked if he was in the Navy due to his life preserver?)

Barry was a little shy, but friendly.

"Hi! You are Laura!"

"That's me," I said happily.

"Coffee?"

"Oh, tea for me, thanks. Just a little milk in it. Shall I hold the table?"

He nodded, bought us hot drinks and came over to join me. I got a crick in my neck just gazing up at him. He made himself comfy and we grinned at each other. I just liked him – it was that simple. So far, so good.

But then, neither of us could find a damn thing to say. After we determined that we'd both found the place just fine, and parked easily, and that his coffee was very nice and my tea was very nice, then, there was... nothing.

Zero. Squat. Nada. Zilch.

Oh my goodness, I am the chatterbox – I'm never at a loss for words! So, I fell back on my trusty little list of questions I had brought with me in my head. This is essential. I'd discovered you must have at least three questions that pertain to the person's life as you'd read it on his profile, or discovered in your first phone conversation. These can be a lifeline to getting through those pauses. A bit of well-placed piffle can keep the oxygen from being sucked right out of the room.

I asked about the house he'd bought, so he launched into his tale. He had found a run-down house, small, circa 1870's fixer-upper, in which he was now camping while he renovated it, a bit at a time. He told me of his love of simple furniture and architecture, his attraction to a very basic rustic style. I felt a little disappointed, as Kurt and I loved a very open, elegant style of architecture, and had collected some wonderful Chinese and Tibetan furniture. Still, I thought quickly, this doesn't have to be a deal breaker. Barry seemed such a nice guy.

He said he could take me, right then, to show me the house if I was interested. My common sense shouted, no, not yet. I explained that I had to get back as I had a client appointment soon, so we just stayed put and chatted on.

A hesitant conversation about alternative medicine turned out to be a non-starter. He knew little to nothing about my field, and had even less interest. His eyes glazed over. Furthermore, he was not a gardener – the only shrub he knew was a rhododendron, and that only because he'd had to hack one down that had recently graced the front entranceway of the new-old house he had just purchased. He said he had hauled it out by the roots and poured gravel at the foundation, instead. I must have visibly cringed.

Oh, dear. Then, bad to worse... He had no interest in self-improvement or the spiritual path, believing it was all flaky, new-age hokum. Now, it might be, the jury is still out, even for me. But, things for Barry and me were not looking good.

One more try. I asked him what music he liked. Jazz. Progressive, unstructured jazz. Musicians I had never heard of. Don't panic, yet, Laura. Then he got to classical music. Not his glass of beer, really (his words, not mine). That killed it. I didn't even bother to tell him of my love of Soft Country, New Age or Celtic music. And, I was afraid if I mentioned harpsichord concertos, he'd damage the doorway as he hurtled out. My poor brain pictured Barry sprinting toward his truck, with a doorframe hung around him like a hula-hoop.

Even after all of this, believe it or not, he asked if we could meet for dinner, sometime soon, at which time he could show me the house as well. He was longing to try the new Indian restaurant that had opened in Newtown, his eyes lighting up as he described the wonders of completely, inordinately, mind-numbingly, tongue-seeringly, over-the-top spicy, hot food. I hate spicy, hot food, and can't find much to eat in an Indian restaurant after the water. For me, blazingly hot food is painfully pointless. After the first mouthful, when I have stopped crying, I can't taste a damn thing since an entire layer of skin and my taste buds have been seared off.

I said I'd have to check my calendar and get back to him. I mentally penciled him in for a Wednesday evening in May, 2038.

By this time, in the online dating arena, I was supposed to be in Stage Three, where you have learned to employ some common sense and find some commonality with the person. But, nope. I had regressed. Sigh. I had taken a nosedive back into Stage Two, where you plunge forward speedily and full of hope and delusion, only to waste both your time and energy and hope in the process. And his as well. Just sayin'.

I knew better. My bad. My own fault for not being more rigid in meeting only people who seemed to be well and truly on my wavelength.

As we walked out, he exclaimed, "Oh, Laura, I've just come from an antique shop where I found the most perfect coffee table. Wait 'till you see it!"

He was nearly drooling. I smiled my encouragement.

He dropped the tailgate on his green Ford F-150, and there stood what appeared to be a pile of crumbling boards held together with rusty nails. I waited for him to move it, so I could see the table.

But, all I got was a beckoning, expectant smile as he swept his arm towards the "table." He stopped just short of saying, "Ta-da!"

Oh. My. All I saw was an ugly, old, cheap piece of junk. Small, beat up, simple to the point of ridiculous. No fine lines, nothing unusual or remotely elegant about it. The truck was more antique than this thing.

"What are you going to do with it, how are you going to fix it up?" I asked politely, still aiming for enthusiasm, but fearing I was failing badly.

Barry stared at me as though I had just grown Shitakes from my ears. He was shocked, and our complete different wavelengths became stunningly and painfully apparent.

"It's perfect, just the way it is. I'm so lucky to find it. I wouldn't change it in any way," he sputtered. "It's 'shabby chic.'"

Like that explained it. Well, I'd always wondered about that expression – "Shabby Shit" was more like it, in my viewpoint. How did we get to the point that crap was cool and worn was wonderful? I would not pick that thing up if someone had left it at the side of the road. If it were free. If someone *paid* me to take it. Nope.

I knew it was hopeless.

I blurted out, "Oh, I see." Of course I didn't. That was all I could say. A brief silence. We looked at each other like the other was a newcomer to this planet. From Pluto.

He suggested, again, that I get in touch regarding dinner, and I, for once, didn't hesitate or beat about the bush.

"You know, it has been great meeting you, but we clearly don't have much in common... Don't you agree?"

He looked a bit surprised, but shrugged. We shook hands and went our separate ways.

Funny, because I didn't feel creepy or uncomfortable about it. It was all part of my learning curve. Nice man, but we lived in completely different worlds. I wouldn't be comfortable in his, and he would never ever fit in mine.

So there you are. Can't win 'em all.

I certainly wasn't winning any of them.

> ***Linus:*** *That's life, Charlie Brown.*
> *You win some, you lose some.*
> ***Charlie Brown****: "Gee, that'd be great."*
> ~ Peanuts cartoon, Charles Schultz

Chapter 19

The Player

"A great many people fall in love with or feel attracted to a person who offers the least possibility of a harmonious union."
~ Dr. Rudolf Deicers

If it seems too good to be true, it is.

There, I don't have to tell you anything more; that one statement says it all. Oh, but no, I will go on. Having decided to reveal the bare, ugly truth, I will.

I was taken in.

Allow me to introduce the pathological liar, the player. A player is like narcotic smoke that creeps and insinuates into the cracks in your psyche – it feels very good for a while and then it makes you ill.

I guess, considering how many men I met, odds are I would meet one. Now that it's behind me, I can't believe I fell for such lies, or gave this man the benefit of the doubt. I had been very fortunate in my life up to that point, having never met a player. I had been in a marriage and other long-term relationships with men I had met in my line of work, or through friends. So I'd escaped the trap.

Rick offered up a piece of information four times, no less, and that should have told me something. He told me he was **not a player.** Uh-huh. It did not dawn on me that, of course, that was exactly what he was. Why did he need to keep telling me he was **not** a player?

I learned, the hard way, the signs of this sad user, this game-playing, time-absorbing demon. Perhaps I can save you some potential heartache or humiliation.

He lived nearby in Fairfield and his profile announced that he was a divorced professional, who wanted a woman "incapable of deception," who would enjoy, "a dedicated and devoted man." That sounded like heaven to me, like sweet honey and maple syrup to this starving girl. He was tall, at 6'3, handsome and rugged looking, and after an email or two, we chatted on the phone.

Even though I was a little shy and my self-worth was lower than Barry White's voice, I had that "gift of gab." So, I was good at breaking the ice. I think it was the fact that we moved endlessly from place to place when I was a kid. Perhaps, it made me develop a charming exterior, to cover the nerves, inside. I can always think up something to say, and I can usually make people laugh.

It was easy, with Rick. It was comfortable and fun on the phone. He was very complimentary about my pictures, my profile, and said he'd love to meet me. So, we agreed to meet the next day at a coffee house in downtown Fairfield.

I had little to no expectations when I drove down to meet him. Having done this a dozen times by this time, I felt like an old hand. No one had remotely gotten to me. I'd enjoyed a few interesting conversations, met a couple of nice people, and met a few strange and bizarre guys, but no one to take home to Ma, as they say! I was feeling dangerously (and prematurely) self-assured. Oh-oh.

I got there a few minutes before our destined time to meet, and finally felt a few nerves begin to grow. Do I get a drink or do I wait? Do I look OK? Will I bore him to death? Will he bore me to death? Has he lied in his profile? Should I just get in my car right now and bag the whole thing?

He walked in the door. Of course, I recognized him straightaway – not many 6'3" guys around. And, he was so much better looking than the photos online. Dramatically so. He was actually rather devastatingly gorgeous. He nailed me between the eyes. I'm not easily nailed.

He acted a little shy. We got our drinks and I set out to make him comfortable, charmed that he was nervous.

"My divorce has just come through," he said, "and I'm new to this dating thing. Not sure what I'm doing, I have to admit!"

I found myself squeezing his arm, to comfort and reassure him. (I failed to realize, then, that he knew *exactly* what he was doing.)

Then, he nailed me again. "I can't believe how beautiful you are," he said.

I grinned. A warm, feeling blossomed deep inside. I felt the beginnings of a gentle sweep off my tired old feet.

"And there's no way you are in your forties. You look like you are 32. Man, oh man, you are just so gorgeous."

"Right back atcha." With my biggest, best smile, I flirted outrageously. Happiness and pheromones bubbled like champagne under my skin, and I felt as if I were floating on air.

This was all so incredibly sweet to my hungry ears, and from there we chatted merrily for two hours, which felt like 20 minutes. We loved the same music, he loved that I played the guitar and sang in my spare time. He asked so many pertinent questions about my life, and listened well. Being totally into health and fitness, he fully appreciated my medical/health background. I learned about his family, his two boys by a marriage when he was only 18, and his 15-year-old son, from a 17-year marriage that had ended three months ago. He even got my Buddhist leanings, when I talked about my goal of reducing the power of the ego.

"Yes, but, it's tough," he said. "I do quite a lot of charity work, but then I get off on it. So much for reducing the ego."

I couldn't believe it. Most people didn't understand what I was talking about when I described the ego as the limiting factor to our spiritual progress. But he did. Immediately. I was blown away.

We could have talked all day, and only an appointment that he had to get to cut our time short.

Outside by my car, he gave me a kiss on the cheek.

"Can I see you for dinner soon?" He asked politely and with a touch of diffidence.

Could he ever! Oh, yes please. In addition, breakfast after that. (Now, now, Laura, you'd better tell them you're just kidding. You are not that type, and …. Oh shut up, put a sock in it, woman, just tell the story.)

The next day, being Thanksgiving, as it happened, meant other obligations, of course, and I suspected we would not be able to meet until after the holiday weekend. I had been so dreading the holidays. I hated being alone. But, things might be looking up.

He left a message the next day, saying he just couldn't stop thinking about me. He sounded so surprised, and added, "I don't know, I just can't!" I want to tell him not to try! Nicest message I've come home to in many years.

Wow, my mind started fantasizing. What lay ahead... New sexy underwear, maybe a few trips to a tanning salon for a gentle glow, double up on my Pilates workouts.

I left a nice return message (phone tag, sigh) saying I was looking forward to talking to him.

Then, silence. No response. For days.

Was I cool, logical, adult, confident? Nah, I picked it apart, I questioned myself, I second-guessed myself: Ooh, what did I say? Was I too forward, was I not encouraging? Or did I tease him and hurt him? Well, it was the Thanksgiving weekend...

Mortifying, I know.

But, I did wonder why in the hell he backed off.

If something seems too good to be true, it is. It was time to repeat that.

Five days later, he called. He explained that his mother had had a stroke, and I felt foolish for worrying about it. I was solicitous, feeling badly for him. He was so upset.

He popped over on his way back from the hospital, for about an hour. It was great. He was warm, and kind, and gentlemanly, and left after he got a call from his brother. He said he had to meet up with his brothers and sisters regarding his mom, because his brother was flying out the next morning. He told me many details, offered up answers to questions before I could even ask them. (Was all this thought out in advance?)

Of course, I bought it.

We enjoyed a wonderful kiss at the door, and this naive woman fell head over heels in attraction. Bonkers, I fell.

He left, and called the next day to tell me he couldn't focus or concentrate on his work for thinking of me. That I was in every thought of the day. Couldn't wait to see me. He explained he had to spend time at the hospital with his mother, but suggested he could pop over for a little while after his evening visit. I agreed, but told him I'd have to boot him out early as I had a heavy workday ahead.

He didn't come by. I waited. And waited. He didn't even call. All evening.

I have to tell you, I'd never encountered anything like this, so of course I gave him the benefit of the doubt. I was sure he didn't call because his mother had taken a dreadful turn for the worse. Or, had even died. I worried, I waited, and sat there all evening unable to do anything else.

The next day when I returned from my long day in Hartford, there was a message from him.

"Hi gorgeous! It's about 11 a.m., and I have just left the hospital. I've been up all night, and mother may have had another mini stroke. I fell asleep in the chair, haven't even had a chance to change clothes. I couldn't call you from the hospital – they don't want you making cell phone calls... But, I want to see you! Can I come see you tonight? Call me back!"

My first thought was, "Wait a minute... "You couldn't get outside for two minutes to make a cell phone call?" Seriously? And then, "Can I come see you?" Now I know he can't plan very well because of his mom, but we had not even had a date. Come see you? When was he going to ask me out? For dinner, maybe?

I finally started to feel the hair creeping up on the back of my neck. Just like something was Not. Quite. Right.

After this message, I thought to check Match. He'd been active in the last 24 hours. So, he'd had time for *that*.

Then just on a whim, and feeling silly and suspicious, I called the hospital where he'd said his mother was. There was no one registered by that name. Moreover, the visiting hours ended at eight, and the woman on the phone said that was rigid.

I explained that I might have the name wrong, that the patient might be registered there by her maiden name or something. The woman replied there was no one in the ICU that had suffered a stroke in the last four days.

What a complete, unadulterated, pathological liar.

I picked up the phone, got his voicemail (of course). "Rick... I am so worried about your mother, I do hope she is not lying in the gutter somewhere, since she is certainly not in the hospital. You are such a liar... It finally dawned on me that during those evenings you were going to call or come over, and didn't, that you were with one of the other women you are juggling. A woman who *had* bought your line. Since all you want is to get into my pants, I want you to understand that's *never going to happen*. You won't be juggling me. Don't call me again, you sick sorry son of a bitch."

♦ ♦ ♦

Players are not funny. They're users. You aren't a person to a player, you are points in his game. It's dehumanizing.

I never heard from him again, and I certainly didn't want to. I would not have wanted to have any further discussion about this. It would be a complete waste of my time. In my experience, confronting a player is like wrestling in the mud with a pig. Both parties get covered with mud, but only the pig enjoys it.

I had made the mistake of creating an exquisite picture of love and companionship and passion. Because I yearned for it. It was a fantasy. I knew somewhere deep inside it was too good to be true. A little voice deep in my head had wondered right up front about the dramatic messages he'd left on my voicemail. Now, I know that kind of behavior is a dead giveaway.

When you are newly alone, you're vulnerable and it's easy to fall victim to the compliments and lies of a player. So said Francesca, in a sweet effort to make me feel less mortified, less foolish. In actuality, having read more about all this since then, it is hard for anyone, vulnerable or not, to see through the charismatic lies of a player. Players catch out lots of women, every day, every month, every year.

That doesn't help much. How silly, used, humiliated, vulnerable, and dumb did I feel? And angry? I can't begin to tell you.

I wasn't born yesterday. I was reborn the day after I left that final voice message for Rick. I gathered my drooping self-worth up as if it were a gorgeous long skirt of silk and lace, and lifted it out of the muck. Then I replaced it with a full dress of armor, awareness, and a healthy dose of suspicion. Or, at least skepticism.

BOTTOM LINE: Here is what I learned about dealing with a player:

He'll be confident, even bold. Usually, a player will be confident, have great eye contact, and doesn't show the nerves or anxiety you might expect when meeting someone new. (Exceptions, of course: Rick acted all shy and self-deprecating, but that was part of his act. Made him even harder to spot as a player.

He'll come on real fast, then quickly and passionately declare his feelings. Rick waxed lyrical about my eyes, how beautiful I was, how he never meets women that he is attracted to like this, etc. It is very easy to be taken in, charmed, and even thrilled by this sort of attention, especially after a horrible break up.

He'll be amazingly romantic. He will take this part seriously. He wants a home run with you, not just first base.

All words and no action: He'll be a genius at knowing what to say. He may say things you yearn to hear, but he doesn't follow through. It's simple – he's playing you.

You won't meet his friends. The player is a loner, usually. Even if he does have close friends, he doesn't want you to talk with them. They might give him away.

He may be looking for a rush in life, a thrill. Does he love a challenge (including you?) Does he love black diamond skiing, car racing, bungee jumping? Is he craving a high? He wants to get a high from conquering YOU.

I say again, one last time, what I learned the hard way:
If it seems too good to be true, it is.
Some of these dating stories are funny, some are infuriating, and some are downright forging. Character building. I felt great, having told that guy off.
And I earned back some Warrior Woman status.

Chapter 20

The Non-Contenders

"If we meet offline and you look nothing like your pics, you're buying me drinks until you do."
~ Anonymous

Months went by. Years, actually. Five of them. I worked, I lived, I laughed with Hank and Francesca, and from time to time, I despaired of finding a partner. I had waded through so many dating sites and emails and winks and coffee dates until it all became a foamy sea of confusion. It was exhausting, disappointing, disillusioning, disheartening, and yes, sometimes downright weird or funny.

I did get better at it. I did, I promise you. There were less and less bizarre stories, and more and more meetings with nice men who I liked, admired, and with whom I had interests in common.

So there I was, one weekday evening, gazing at my computer yet again, and way beyond sick of it, I can tell you.

The vast majority of men who had profiles on an online dating site are what I called the "Non-Contenders," because you'd never even contact them. Those guys didn't even make the first cut. They are like the little bits floating around the editing room floor. This, of course, is not because there was something wrong with all of them. For most, they had interests completely removed from mine or just didn't appeal to me. And, let's face it, attraction, both physical and psychological, is vital.

Unfortunately, some men are just not your type. For me, I have to 'fess up to having an unfair and irrational prejudice against large front teeth. I realize as I say it, this would preclude me from ever having a fling with a Kennedy, intelligent, charming and powerful though they may be. I do apologize to all chipmunks and other little furry creatures. It is nothing personal. But, front teeth that resemble Arizona butted up against New Mexico, or two giant Chiclets – I just can't do it. I do try hard not to be judgmental in my life... And I know what you're thinking, "How small can you be?" However, I just cannot wake up to a large rodent asleep on the pillow next to me for the rest of my life.

This presents a small problem. If the photo available on the site has no wide smile, enough to show his teeth, you are just not going to be able to tell. What do you do, insist on a picture from each guy that includes a good view of teeth? What kind of shallow clump are you, Laura? Sigh. I do have such a long way to go on the path to enlightenment.

However, sometimes the reason you would never contact someone on an online dating site is pretty damned obvious and much more rational than an obscure prejudice against a squirrelly overbite. There is a vast and inexplicable universe of stupidity presented by the guys who fill out profiles.

For those of you who have looked at Plenty of Fish, OK Cupid, or Match, just three of the many sites, you know that there is only a short blurb of each person visible on the page of your search. There will be ten pictures of ten different guys with a sentence or two visible for each, and the word "more" if you are enticed to keep reading. You have to click to another page. Therefore, it's important to read some useful information about the contestant – I mean competitor – I mean available party – in those first few lines.

It appears that many men don't ever check to see what their profile looks like to a woman searching the site. So many of the men's first sentences said something like, "I don't know where to begin, never having done this before...." Or, "I have no idea what to say about myself," or, "This is really hard – I'm not very good at this, but I'll have a go." One even started off, "Well, there's not really much to say..." I kid you not.

Then you see the little blue underlined link that says *"more."* Why the hell would you click on any of these people's profiles? That's right, dear boy, waste the first three sentences telling me you don't want to be doing this, you don't know how to do it, and you don't like the whole idea anyway. Next.

Then there was the good-looking guy who said, "Have a look at my ugly mug and respond if you are interested." But, there were 28 photos of him in every possible position, in every possible light, various ages, various poses and grins. He sure wanted the viewers to get a chance to see his "ugly mug" from every possible vantage point. He clearly knew he was gorgeous and he enjoyed loading up as many pictures as the site would allow. Self-absorption. Next.

Which brings me to the way people say, "I am good-looking, I have been told." Or, "My friends say I am good looking, charming, smart," or whatever. This means you have absolutely no idea if you are attractive, charming or smart? You need your friends to define you? Come on, people, just tell it like it is. Unless you actually don't know how it is. One man's profile started off like this, "It's hard to describe yourself, your life, your personality while staring at a screen trying to guess what type you are." Can you believe that? You've been marching around a portion of the planet for 40 or 50 years and you don't know who you are? And worse yet, you think telling me this is increasing your chances of a response?

Another interesting type of man was the one who loaded up a fairly decent description of himself, two good photographs, and there was nothing overtly offensive in his written section (oh, how we slacken our criteria when desperate). He talked about his profession, his kids, and what he liked to do for hobbies. Ok, you think, this is not bad, so you keep reading.

But, then I came upon the last paragraph, which "for your information" listed his "brands." His 'brands"? And there they were: Jeep Cherokee, Armani, Starbucks, North Face. Plus, several others I didn't even recognize, because I, apparently, was not as cool as he was. So this is how you like to define yourself? By the crap that you buy? I'm sure he would never have wanted to hear my brands... Tractor

Supply, Dress Barn, WD40, Midol. Hmmm, Oreos. KFC. Nair. For my lip. You get my drift. I do wish I had thought of this at the time – it could have served to filter out the faint of heart.

Another favorite turn-off had to be the men who are either so dumb, or so lazy, that they didn't bother to check their profile for typos, obvious glaring mistakes in grammar, or spelling. He may have waxed lyrical about how he was going to romance you, wine you, dine you, take you for long beach walks in the moonlight (these are rampant, it seems, among single people.) So, I assure you I don't mean any disrespect to the poor little dork filling out his profile who either didn't make it past the fourth grade or didn't think it was necessary to spell-check his invitation to romance. However, I had no intention of responding to him.

Even if he had a PhD, an MBA, or was a lawyer or doctor, those gents weren't much better. It didn't seem to relate to their willingness to take the time to create an attractive profile. It came across to me, the reader, as arrogant, stupid, or showing an amazing lack of real interest in finding someone special, if they didn't even respect the process enough to present something intelligent and well-written.

Next, there is an honorable mention to the arrogant sexist who listed his "ideal woman" as fifteen or more years younger than himself. Didn't he know what a fool he looked for doing that? Maybe he was only interested in bimbos, because that is all who would respond to him.

My vote for priceless example of Really Not Getting the Art of the Online Dating Ad was this gentleman's profile I encountered a few months into my online odyssey. (I have to question the use of the word "gentleman" here). The photo was of a rather goofy-looking individual in a dirty, stained T-shirt, sitting on an unmade bed, rumpled sheets and all. Over his shoulder was the open door inviting us to gaze into his bathroom, where towels graced the floor, and the toilet seat was up. How enticing. It might have been a good idea, buddy, when you set up that timer switch on your digital camera to take a brief gander at the surroundings. And, certainly check that you removed the condom and rumpled tissues from the bedside table.

Finally, there was the extremely brief encounter I had with a "gentleman" (again, I have to *seriously* question his qualifications) who responded to my wink. His email response was short, sharp, and to the point:

"Nice pics, nice profile. GOT ANY MONEY?"

Uh-huh. I swear it is the truth.

After a rather stunned moment, I shot off a quick reply, "This technique WORKS for you?" Then, before I deleted this perturbing little email, I copied and pasted it to a Word document for safekeeping. So, that when I just couldn't believe it had happened, it was there, staring at me in black and white. Proof. Around that time I thought, damn, I must write a book. I couldn't make this stuff up if I tried.

As a postscript, I must add a list of general "no-no's" and deal-breakers that I encountered:

1) Men who loathed their ex, or spent an hour railing against what she did to him. The kind of guy that bragged: "I managed to hide my assets…" Bully for you, I say. You think I'd like to consider you as a potential partner? *Not.*

2) If the attraction was just not there... I learned: *Don't make allowances.* I had to keep telling myself that, as the years of dating went on and on. I learned you just couldn't trust that the attraction would grow. Does that ever actually happen? Rarely, in my experience. I decided I would not wait for attraction, hoping it would spark up further on down the road.

3) Oh, and here's an easy one: Men who were not warm and fuzzy to the waiter. Rudeness to a waiter or waitress is a deal-breaker. Non-negotiable. No matter how polite he is to you in the moment, if he treats anyone else with disrespect, it is only a matter of time before he will turn that on you.

4) And finally, I learned to watch out for: cheapskates, player/playboys, liars, narcissists, and other damaged, dark souls.

I learned to separate the wheat from the chaff. And oh, there was a lot of chaff!

> *"It's right there in the name. It's not 'Great Cupid' or even 'Good Cupid.' It's 'OK Cupid.'"*
> ~ Helen Hong, Comedienne

Chapter 21

New Age Guy
or
True Consciousness

"To me, when I think of New Age, I think of crystals and rainbows and platitudes."
~ Marianne Williamson

Depression had set in a bit fierce. It was all I could do to get up some days. Patients needed me and I needed to pay the rent, so in the end I successfully got my ass out of bed every morning. However, and this is just between you and me, there were a few weekends when I never got out of bed at all. I caved to the lowness.

These times recurred periodically during the five-year saga. But, oddly enough, the internet dating hope got me through. I just couldn't completely squelch the hope. Something told me to keep going, keep trying, keep hoping. That there simply must be someone out there for me that would excite me, challenge me, and with whom I could create a life of love and happiness.

This next guy did not help, it was one more disappointment. His name was Raymond, but I thought of him as "New Age Guy." You know the type: flaky and full of golden-age rainbows. New Age baloney is just baloney, after all.

This man was a little effeminate, and a bit soft and pudgy. He didn't seem to know what he wanted to do when he grew up – he was 49 years old. He told me he loathed material possessions. (But, apparently, he owned a computer...) I like nice things but I don't worship them. This guy wore his asceticism like a crown, sort of a gilded self-denial. The more he proclaimed, the less I believed him. The gentleman "doth protest too much, methinks."

If he despised material possession, could this be because he'd never managed to acquire any of them? Sometimes people justify their lives if they can't create the kind of success they secretly desire. They simply decide it isn't important to them and claim a whole ton of spiritual justification for their limited possessions.

Was New Age Guy's identity wrapped up in his poverty? He waffled on, over coffee, about giving things up and becoming monk-like. This would mean no identity, no ego whatsoever, no self- worth. He claimed we all needed to "give up the self."

Actually, between you and me, the bottom line? He seemed like a needy loser.

Sorry, I know that's harsh, and I'm supposed to be kind, and loving and all that good stuff.

As I drove home from this disappointing meeting, it suddenly hit me. Like a ton of bricks. Wow, I thought. Look at how I reacted to that poor soul. I'm so damned judgmental! I abhor that in other people! But, I guess it's true.

You are thinking, "Duh."

Where was my compassion? Who was I to judge? Why did I react so harshly (if not overtly, then certainly privately)? Part of it was the heartbreak, even though a good deal of time had now passed, it seemed to have created some scar tissue in my heart.

I had stopped seeing the good in people. Why? Was I looking for the bad because of what Kurt did to me? Was I expecting it? Was I now guilty of the dreaded don't-ever-trust-anyone-again syndrome?

There was also a deeper truth I just couldn't avoid any longer. From time to time, I had suspected that it might have been right, or better for me, somehow, if I had expressed true anger for what Kurt did. Appropriate anger. The anger that Francesca could not believe I didn't feel. Within a day or two of his leaving, I had excused him, said things like, "If he is not happy, he needs to go." And, "I love him, therefore I want his well-being and happiness. Therefore I want for him what he wants for himself."

OK, sounds good. But I just wasn't that holy, that angelic, that evolved, that saintly! Nice try, Laura. Truth is, I had suppressed all that anger and it popped out from time to time in nastiness toward other people – poor innocent men I interacted with from dating sites. It was only shared with Francesca, or Hank, not the men themselves, but still, that does not make it right.

That anger had grown over the years. I was damned angry with him for letting me down! He had promised me a lifetime of love and romance. He said he would never leave me. We were supposed to be happy in our new house in Connecticut. Instead, I was alone, trying to meet people.

And I didn't want to be alone.

Each time the dating process let me down, my expectations, hope, and patience were worn down as well. The anger grew and grew, although I did not acknowledge it for a long time. My brain finally acknowledged, "He's the reason I have to do this. If he hadn't left me, I wouldn't be stuck playing whack-a-mole."

So all those guys suffered my misdirected wrath. Wrath at Kurt. But he got off scot-free.

I realized I needed to make a conscious effort to open my heart, to practice less judgment and true compassion. I had been talking the talk, sure, but it was clearly time for me to walk the talk as well.

My main motto in life had been, for many years, before Kurt: "It is better to be loving than it is to be right." Doesn't that sound just downright Mother Teresa-ish? I ask you.

I needed to make my way back to that. With some additions. Maybe: "Love with all your passion, be kind with all your heart, laugh with all your might, and stay out on the dance floor."

Or, more succinctly, I will quote William Shakespeare, "Love all, trust a few, do wrong to none."

Chapter 22

I Give the Hell Up

*Sometimes there is nowhere else to go
but down... on our knees.*

Five years had passed. I had met 87 guys for a cup of coffee, and only a few for anything beyond that. Two or three lunches, two or three dinners, one relationship that did not work out. Those years had not passed easily, but were rather like carrying a suitcase full of bricks on my head and trying to walk across mainland China.

Now, I was filled with the sensation that I had fallen all the way to the bottom of a deep, dark well. I had reached the lowest of the low. It was just never going to work. Here I'd thought I was going to be the loving life-mate and partner to a wonderful guy, but no, I was going to be alone, forever, the old lady naturopath with a slew of cats, a lavender garden and a fine collection of unmatched (but antique) English bone china cups and saucers.

The closest I came during this long five years was spending several months seeing Pete, a very nice man who moved to Los Angeles for a great job promotion. So, we broke up. I was not going to move to southern California, and besides, this man had no concept of "team." He'd been married once, and apparently, that had been enough. He never wanted to marry again, and I wanted a real team connection. A collaboration. A one-and-one-makes-three relationship. A pie-plate team. It was never right with Pete. So, I waved him good-bye, and after a few sad, sorry-for-myself, drink-a-bit-too-much-Zaya-rum evenings, I climbed back on the Marry-Go-Round of online dating.

I whined at the universe: Damn it, I have been determined, tenacious, and patient (mostly), for five freaking years.

Oh, and there were a few other challenges in my life. First, of course, as I have described, I had to move my practice, after watching, helplessly, as the wonderful folks who owned the clinic where I worked go bankrupt. My practice then dropped in half, mostly thanks to the Great Recession of 2008, which also ate 25% of my tiny investment portfolio. Now I would have to work until I was 85.

Then, I waded through the nightmare that is breast cancer with my older sister, Katie, with a positive outcome, thank heavens. It was deeply scary. I took time off work to take her to appointments, and visited her often during her time in the hospital. And oh, the hours I spent trying to buoy up Frank, her husband. Poor, terrified man.

All this gives you a new perspective on the time we have here, when you are forced to seriously contemplate your sister's potential demise. To stare with her into the abyss. And then your own mortality jumps up and screams in your face, as well. It slams home how fragile this life is.

But, she did just great and my eyes fill with tears every time I think of it. Mastectomy and radiation later, she went into remission, and the whole family breathed hesitant, hopeful sighs of relief. This story, of course, is a book in itself.

During this time, I also orchestrated the sale of my mom's house, where she had lived for 40 years, 30 of which were with my father. Helping her sort things out and move to a tiny apartment, I found myself wading with her through her fears, her sadness at moving, and her grief at having to part with so many memories. I felt so badly for her. I didn't even need to hunt for patience with her "over-talking," with her fear of silence. She was hurting. And lonely.

As you can see, it was a series of banner, joy-filled years. You know the old saying that nasty events come in threes? Well, these life challenges felt more as if a cupful of manure dropped on my head as a mini prelude to the dump-truck load or two right behind it.

Of course, throughout all this, I marched relentlessly on in the online dating mess, hoping to find my true partner. It turned out to be the ultimate exercise in polishing one's patience. While hoping it would all pay off.

So here I was, once again, back on Match, but this time I'd signed up for one month only. Enough was enough. I was ready to gracefully concede defeat. Just kidding. It was not going to be graceful. I longed to have back the gas money that had gone into five years of driving to meet guys for pointless cups of coffee.

For a couple of weeks, I poodled around on the site, but my heart was not in it. Not at all. At the two-weeks-left mark, there I was, once again using up my evening to stare at the computer screen. I was seeing the same people on these dating sites, over and over again! Some may have had relationships that failed, and were back on again. Others had been on for months or years, unsuccessfully, I guess. Others were men with whom I had communicated or met and it had not been right. Ok, maybe I should just pull the plug, quit, finish, and sign off, end the entire, miserable, depressing catastrophe.

Suffering one of the worst migraines, ever, didn't help. One of those right-sided kebab forks through my eye. Those of you familiar with the joys of migraines know of which I speak: the skewer that pins you through the eye right out the back of your head and into the pillow beneath you. The headaches that are so bad that you can't watch TV, read, have a conversation, eat, or do anything but hang on and breathe as well as you can through the damn thing.

I saw all this as a sign that I was done. Maybe I would just cancel out and leave the last two weeks...

I turned off my laptop.

I snuggled down in my leather chair with Pusskin on my lap and sighed. I was tired. Tired of it all: the searching, the believing, the hoping, the trying, the being alone, the getting up and dusting myself off again and again. I felt like Mrs. Sisyphus, pushing the giant dating boulder up the hill every day, just to feel it tumble back down, back down over my life, every night.

Or, I felt I had been treading water for five long years. I was now waterlogged, and wrinkled as a prune. Afraid I had learned nothing, gained nothing, was no wiser.

I'd been through so many struggles. I'd lost heart and faith a little, I'd cried a lot, tried a lot, I'd fought and screamed and it was time to relax. Give it up, girl. Realize you don't have a clue and then just take a deep breath. Be mindful of right now, I told myself. The fire was crackling away in front of me, warming my stockinged toes. Pusskin stretched out like a sphinx all the way to my ankles, her shiny black fur sparkling gold in the firelight.

I clicked off the TV, which, although muted, had been injecting its flashing, harsh images into my consciousness.

Ah, that's better. I warmed a brandy glass with the palms of my hands, swirling a touch of Courvoisier around and around, and found myself admiring the caramel-colored liquid. I breathed in its heady fragrance, then took a sip and felt it slip warm and vibrant, all the way down.

Let it be. Surrender. Let go and let God. It is what it is.

Maybe with capitulation came a sort of resignation, which I prefer to call acceptance, as it sounds better. Acceptance. A big word, in every sense. Although we learn what it means and how to spell it in about the fourth grade, what a huge lesson it is to take in fully, to really *get*. To truly accept. To trust.

Perhaps it can save you in the dark night of the soul, to know that change will, inevitably, occur. That the only thing you can count on is change. Sometimes when things look horribly dark, when there is nowhere lower to crawl, or to fall, to know deep down inside you that the only way left is up.

Or down on your knees.

I dropped my head back on the headrest of my wonderful chair, and felt supported. I was warm. I was content. I closed my eyes and took in this moment.

I was actually happy.

At that moment, I felt a warm feeling in my chest, a radiating energy, a vibrant but gentle awareness... Of what? My own spirit? I can't explain it, even today, but something shifted. That's the best I can do to explain it. There was a shift. Deep inside me. My heart seemed to expand outward, get larger, until I felt an energy radiating outward to every cell in my body. I could feel the blood running in my veins, and I felt alive, yet calm. My muscles and bones felt part of that energy wave. My brain wanted to jump around and try to analyze the whole thing, to put it into words, but I held it steady, from my years of meditation practice.

Wait, be still. Stay here. Do nothing. Do not think.

Be still.

Pusskin felt the energy. I felt her move a little and heard her little questioning "Mrrr?" I touched her gently. "I know, little one. It's all right."

She settled under my touch, and once again, I closed off my thoughts to analysis and just enjoyed the moment. It felt like a reward. To finally understand that there was nothing I had to do, nothing I had to be, nothing I had to succeed at, nothing I had to find. Everything was perfect and fine and I was blessed, right here in this precious moment.

The giant yawning pit that had haunted me for several years seemed a long distance behind me, now. I no longer feared that the hellish chasm would widen, would stretch out to engulf me in this moment. No longer afraid it would open, and swallow me up.

I no longer feared it at all.

In that moment, I felt as close to God as I could feel.

Chapter 23

One Last Try

"Lookin' for love in all the wrong places
Lookin' for love in too many faces" ♪
~ Songwriters: Bob Morrison,
Patti Ryan, Wanda Mallette

"My whole life changed the day I told my long deceased father to go fuck himself."

What? My first thought was, what is it with this place? Did someone actually say that? I was in Stop and Shop, at the deli counter, again, awaiting the wonders of sliced turkey that someone else had cooked and prepared. A wonder in itself. Noodling around with the notion of completely redoing my kitchen, counters and all, my mind had been miles away in Italian ceramic-tile-land.

I chuckled to myself. The mousy woman nearby had spoken in hushed, yet proud tones to her friend. I shifted a little to my right, hoping to hear more.

At that moment a voice hollered out, "Number 42, number 42!"

Damn. It was certainly the first time in my life, waiting for anything, that I didn't want my number to be called.

As I collected my order and thanked the guy at the counter, I stole a quick glance at the two women, now collecting their own deli goodies. Unfortunately, I guess I was never going to know the rest of the story. I grinned, and turned my cart toward the checkout.

Oh, wait, I know. Maybe the woman had been talking about her therapy. Perhaps her therapist had suggested she imagine her father sitting in a chair opposite her, and she should tell him how she truly felt. Yes, that was it. Having undergone therapy at various intervals throughout my life, I was relatively familiar with the tricks of the trade. On the other hand, maybe she'd been to a medium, her father had appeared to her in some fashion, and she had finally let him have it. Well, good for her! I guess...

"Hey, Laura!"

I heard Francesca's voice, and spotted her coming towards me up the bread aisle.

"Hey honey!" I said. Always so nice to see her beautiful self. "Oh, I should have told you I was headed to the store – I could have picked up things for you."

She waved off that comment and studied my face. "What's up with you? You look tired."

"Oh," I said. "I've just recovered from the Mother of All Migraines. Feel like I've been in a head-on collision with an 18-wheeler. It won."

"Oh, sweetie, that's horrible. You poor dear, I wish you could find something that works for those migraines besides drugs."

"Yeah, but thank heavens for sumatriptan. That stuff is magical. Now, don't tell anyone I said that. Bad for my naturopathic image."

Francesca grinned. "There is something I want to talk to you about. This online dating –"

I cut her off. "Nope. I am Done."

"I know, I know, honey. And I can't convince you to keep trying..."

"You can't."

She continued. "But I've been thinking about it. You have two weeks left. Shame to waste them."

I rolled my eyes.

Francesca gave a small, wry smile. "Hear me out. You told me you have set a 50-mile radius... And, specified Divorced or Never Married, right?"

I nodded.

"Well, that gives you a ton of people to wade through, and a lot you've already seen, right?"

Intrigued and wondering where she was going, I just nodded again.

"Well, I think you should widen your radius to 75 miles. Just for this last two weeks. And specify 'Widowed Only.'"

The 75 miles made sense, even though it was a bit exhausting to contemplate. But, I must have looked somewhat puzzled.

"Widowed men are less apt to be damaged than divorced guys," she explained. "And the 'Never Marrieds,' well, why would you think men in their forties or fifties who have never committed to marriage would be great team partners?"

She paused, in thought for a moment. "A widower is more apt to believe in marriage, in being part of a team. His wife didn't choose to leave the relationship – she did not hurt him, intentionally. She left because she had no choice. It changes the way you feel and how you view relationships."

I pondered that. "It's true, what a good point. You have a cleaner view of love and relationships, don't you?"

She nodded. Then smiled a small, perhaps nostalgic smile. "William didn't leave me on purpose. He didn't cheat on me, grow tired of me, or hurt me. He just died. Maybe you can find someone who believes in love and marriage..."

Francesca was amazing. What a great idea. She is so gracious with her wisdom. And kindness.

And it was only two weeks, after all.

I was dubious. And beyond tired of the whole thing.

"As long as I am not trying to compete with a saint."

Francesca laughed. "Oh, come on now, you are just being negative. Give it a try, please? If it doesn't work, you can give up and hang around the organic veggie aisle at Whole Foods, OK? I'll come with you!"

That sounded like fun. Love over a rutabaga?

◆ ◆ ◆

Having stashed away the groceries and eaten a light, healthy dinner of wild salmon and basmati rice, I parked myself back down in front of the computer. Francesca's idea had come at the right moment: two weeks left and I might as well try something different.

I was feeling positive. After my big "moment" of calm and peace the night before, I had slept like a baby. The next morning I had come to another realization: I needed to choose life. I needed to make life the best that I could make it. It might not consist of my magnificent dream of a perfect partner, but life was still good. It held the promise of moments of sweetness, it was full of potential moments of happiness.

So onwards and upwards!

I logged in. (Damn, I knew this site so well I could have taught tutorials in its use, I thought, and chuckled to myself.)

I widened my search filter so that it included 75 miles distant from my zip code, instead of the 50 miles I had chosen when this odyssey began. And, I asked for just widowed men, not divorced, not still single.

What the hell.

I pressed Enter, and presto, a page with the customary 18 pictures lined my screen. I glanced at the first man... nope. Seen him before.

But, the second image. Hmmm. He was 65 miles away, which of course is why I hadn't seen him before. Now, he was interesting. Clicking through to see more pictures and read his profile text, I glanced at the half a dozen photos he had shared. What a warm smile. A slightly gray beard and mustache (oh yum), and handsome features. Not too young, which I like – he was 53, so a little older than I was. One photo caught my eye, of him with a group of people, probably family, at a wedding. He wore a beautiful gray suit, and that great smile.

I started to read. Oh, what a thoughtful, intelligent man. A veterinarian, he had built his own clinic practice about 65 miles from me, in West Hartford. He described himself as a naturalist, loving the outdoors, and there were images of a beautiful round garden he had created at his home, which he called his Medicine Wheel Garden. He loved dogs – of course – the man was a vet! As for music, he listed classical and country music among other genres he appreciated. Our views on politics and spirituality seemed well aligned, at least as much as you can tell from reading a profile.

OK, let's give it a shot, I thought. Maybe I'd find a like-minded companion with whom I'd enjoy concerts. I'd always loved artsy West Hartford and it wasn't that far.

I popped a quick email to him that said, simply, in the subject, "Love your beard!" After a couple of friendly lines about enjoying his profile text, I moved on to scan through the other profiles this new search had turned up.

I didn't get far.

Within ten minutes, I heard a ping and there was an email. From him.

The subject line read, "Looked at your pictures. Read your profile. Marry me." Inside the email it started, "Well, maybe one date first."

I laughed and thought that either I'd bowled him over, or he was mildly insane.

I hoped for the former.

Over the next two or three days we exchanged quite a few emails sharing details and history. I grew more and more intrigued. His name was Michael, my favorite man's name. Suzanne, his wife, had passed away from the dreaded ovarian cancer, way too young. He spoke so glowingly about her that I had to quell the little doubting voice whispering from the back of my mind, trying to scare me off.

His emails were witty, warm, complimentary towards me, and not pushy. It was I who suggested we speak on the phone, so we set up a time.

And, what a call it was! Three hours on the phone, no less. First of all, there was his voice, deep, rich, and warm. The kind of voice that melts you all the way down to your toes. He told me of his escapades into the world of voice-over acting, and had me rolling on the floor with laughter, with his delightful Irish sense of humor. Don't you just love a sense of humor that is not at someone else's expense? I do so appreciate that.

We chatted about our work, his English Setters, Alison Kraus, the Romantic poets and Kahlil Gibran, and his wonderful round garden. He talked about Carrie, his beautiful daughter, and her ability to make everyone laugh.

Then, I found myself offering up a little of the sorry state of my last relationship. Up to this point, when meeting people, I had played it down. But, the mess with Kurt was finally feeling like history, not current trauma. It was becoming easier to talk about.

Having agreed to meet for coffee half way on the next Saturday, we finally hung up the phone.

I felt a bit dizzy, disoriented. I realized I was falling for the essence of this person. I was charmed, in the nicest possible way. I just liked him so much, so far! I reminded myself he might be 5'6", have two noses, be 83, or be a lying, narcissistic player.

But, somehow, I didn't think so.

Geez, Laura, don't be seduced by the poetic, here, girl. Don't think too much about it, don't read anything into it. If you meet a friend, that would be a lovely gift.

But, it felt like love at first insight.

Chapter 24

Michael

"I had always thought that the idea of love at first sight was one of those things invented by lady novelists from the South with three names."
~ John Perry Barlow

So, I hear you ask, "Was it love at first sight?"

I will answer that by saying it was a moment like no other.

Driving to meet him, I carried on quite a conversation. With myself. Mostly one-sided, the discussion originated from that voice inside me attempting to keep me calm, and telling me to get a grip, basically.

That voice reminded me:

"There is something wrong with all of them."

"You have had the love of your life with Kurt, and you probably don't get to have it twice."

"There could be zero chemistry."

"He could be a freak."

Even if he is the perfect man – I laughed aloud on I-84 at that thought – don't forget, Laura, there is still the whole angelic wife piece to process and handle, graciously. Yikes.

Oh, Laura, just let it be, let it flow, don't expect anything at all.

I pulled into the shopping mall, parked a row or two away from Starbucks, and headed for the door, navigating some ice and snow underfoot on that February Saturday. I remember exactly what I was wearing: my best snug black jeans, red turtleneck sweater and a warm jacket with a furry collar. Dangly red earrings. Hair curled to look like it never needed it. Soft makeup job, but red lips to match the sweater. Plus, heeled boots that I know gave me a sway of the hips. The kind men like.

Then I saw him. And the moment began. Time slowed as the first impression carved a brand on my soul. Tall, with a full head of dark graying hair, jeans and cowboy boots, black turtleneck and soft leather jacket.

But, it was the smile. That smile that still brings tears to my eyes, here and now, as I write this. The warmth, the welcome, the crinkle around those gorgeous gray-blue eyes.

The moment moved me right up to him. I stopped, his arms came around me, and I gave him a soft kiss on the lips. Brief and as natural as spring rain. As sweet as a daffodil. As right as a newborn baby's heart.

I saw the surprise in his eyes, from the kiss, but not shock.

Later it hit me how out of character that was for me. Why on earth did I kiss a man I'd never even met? But, at the time, it was absolutely right.

"Hi."

One of us said it first, I now have no idea who. We stood there for a long time – was it a minute, was it an hour? – looking in each other's eyes, and he later confessed he was so blown away by that same moment in his soul that he couldn't find anything at all to say.

Nothing needed to be said.

Then, the moment broke, and we talked over a cup of coffee... for five hours.

Michael and I bypassed dating and launched straight into romance, togetherness, connection, team partnership, love, and marriage. We haven't been apart for more than a couple of nights at a time, ever since. This did not feel impulsive, wrong, or stupid. It was natural and right.

He wanted what I wanted: to be part of a team. To love so much, so well, so completely, that you can honestly say, "What happens to you, happens to me."

As for me, I had decided, late in this five-year trek, to allow myself to be vulnerable again, when it felt right. As I healed, I decided to allow myself to truly love again. Because if you hold back, it is not real love. I heard somewhere, "Real love is giving someone the power to hurt you." That's so true, isn't it? Letting yourself be vulnerable after having been so hurt may be the hardest thing to do. But I had decided to do it, and it paid off. Like the lottery.

Our first night? Rather than attempt to describe it in narrative, I will simply share the poem I wrote at the time.

This beautiful long, long night

To experience this night of bliss,
to rest in each other's love and acceptance
and feel the joy of our connection.
To feel God and the love of the universe
expand in our hearts and souls.
While you hold me, cover my lips with yours,
you fill me with your spark of life.
I devote all my source to you and us,
until a million stars and a million flowers
shower us with light and fragrance.
The power of home and love and beauty and joy
smoothes the tears from our cheeks,
the pain from our hearts,
and soothes our soul,
easing the aching of missing, of longing, of desire.
It is quiet. No need to talk,
we are already fully sharing.
This night!
Lost and found in the moment
Lost in you and found in me
The Now, the exhilarating Now.
In this beautiful long, long night

Epilogue

4 years later

*"A happy marriage is a long conversation
which always seems too short."*
~ Andre Maurois

It is incredible to look back on these four years, and each day fills me with heartfelt gratitude.

It was a glorious first few months together and we married before a full year had passed. Although his mother warned him about moving too quickly, saying, "Be careful," his younger brother, Luke, replied, "Nah, Ma, he's *OLD*. He doesn't have time to be careful."

As for me, I tried, of course, to hold back. I knew that, from my experience, those first feelings of "love" are actually attraction and romantic attachment caused by oxytocin and fantasy. This holding back attempt lasted, oh, maybe a week.

He told me, early on, that he was going to break all records for how many times a man can kiss a woman. He is succeeding.

Who is Michael? He is a strong man. And, although physically this is true, (my gorgeous hunk) I mean this in a much deeper, broader way. He knows what it means to be a man; he takes action and solves problems, in the best male sense. He knows his strength and uses it to take care of me, his family, his home. There is not one ounce of bully in him.

While he is indeed strong, in the male ways I described, he admires, even cherishes the feminine. He admires and cherishes *me*, and shows me every day. He enjoys his feminine side, and supports it, knowing it strengthens rather than weakens him.

He feeds the creative, which is where I live and breathe. It was exciting and rewarding for me to find another soul who believes that while mankind may be capable of unspeakable acts of evil and violence, we offer ourselves redemption by the creation of divine beauty, such as art, music, and poetry.

He introduced me to Walter Benton, who wrote the most romantic, soul-searing poetry I have ever experienced. Tucked up together in front of the fire, Michael and I read to each other from Benton's exquisite book of poems, *This is My Beloved.* There is just nothing more deliciously romantic on earth than reading poetry aloud to the one you love.

The first time we went to a chamber music concert, I chose Bach's Violin Concerto in D minor. There is a slow movement in that piece that is so exquisite I almost cannot stand it. I am moved deeply by such glorious music, to the point that Bach's heavenly melodies begin to run along the river of my blood, and simply take me over. At one such moment in this concert, Michael squeezed my hand, and when I turned to meet his eyes, I discovered that they, too, were full of tears.

The exact same thing happened later that summer at an open-air Alison Krauss concert, when she sang "Looking in the Eyes of Love."

Soul mates? Maybe.

And, he's as funny as they come! Few days have passed in this last four years that he didn't make me laugh. Usually multiple times a day. There was the time we were driving back from a wonderful Italian dinner and I was explaining why I didn't want to have dessert. Even though it was the heavenly Crème Brule, which tempts me like no other, I just couldn't eat another bite. Besides, a lifetime of watching calories had kicked in as well. Joking, I said, "I just can't eat that, the anorexic in me won't let me."

Quick as a flash he replied, "I have an anorexic in me, too. I ate one last week."

Michael looks after me and I look after him. He loves and gets the concept of team being the pie-plate. He told me I could trust him, and that I would never be sorry I loved him. I believe him. He is the most honorable man I have ever known.

He does not criticize me. He supports me 100%, no matter what. Add to that the traits of faithfulness, loyalty, courage, compassion, and intelligence and you begin to see what a lucky, blessed woman I am to have found him.

What about the whole something-wrong-with-all-of-them piece? Well, no one is perfect, and Michael has his flaws. I will not mention them here, as they are not even worth mentioning. This is because he has been working on himself his entire adult life; he works to be the best man he can be. I so admire him for that!

As for the years of online dating, and all the trials and tribulations of my life, my path, the struggles, I came to a realization. It is expressed perfectly in the country song, "Bless the Broken Road." *"God bless the broken road that led me straight to you."* Oh, yes. All the broken bends and twists of my life had led me to Michael.

Do I think fate played a hand? I have absolutely no idea. I do know that had I done anything differently, if I had made other choices along the way, I would not have found him.

I could finally, in my heart, thank Kurt for leaving me.

As for Match and all the other dating sites, Michael and I both signed off within a few days of meeting each other. And, as unfair as it may seem, while I had slogged relentlessly, even obstinately through the online dating process for five long years, Michael had endured it for an entire *two weeks*. Oh, the poor, patient soul. He had met one woman, who he described as pleasant, but not interesting enough to him to pursue. He had signed up for six months worth of Match, but later complained to me that he wanted his money back for the five and a half months he didn't use. He amuses new friends with our online dating story, telling them he was on the sale rack and I'd bought him cheap.

He loves being a husband. He is good at it. In the first weeks of getting to know him, I learned from his daughter about the kind of husband he had been to her mother. Carrie is the sort of vibrant, outgoing person who does not even know about self-worth issues. She was loved, respected, and supported her whole young life. She fills a room with her personality, born leader that she is.

And she adores her dad.

She was over for dinner, and she and I were together in the kitchen, cleaning up, while Michael and her fiancé, Jason, cleaned the grill outside on the deck.

"How long have you and Jason been together?" I asked her. I know that was a bit personal, but Carrie is such a warm and open person, and had been so welcoming to me, that it was easy to talk with her.

"Oh, forever, it seems."

"And getting married was just a natural evolution?"

"For the last few years, Jason has asked me to marry him about 47 times." Carrie laughed as she dried the big pot in which we'd made rice. A strand of long, dark hair had escaped the band of her ponytail, and she tucked it behind her ear. "I have probably hurt him a bit, the dear soul, because I kept refusing for the longest time."

"Why?" She was only 23, so I figured she had just wanted to play the field for a while, and not settle down too early.

Carrie put down the towel and the pot. She turned to me and spoke slowly. "I explained it to Dad, when he asked a while ago... All those years I kept turning Jason down because, as a husband, Dad set the bar so high, I thought Jason would never measure up." She paused, and smiled at me. "I finally said yes because I realized that no one ever could."

Yes, this is my Michael. He set the bar so high that most other men could not reach it even if they stood on their tiptoes.

And oh, how I love him!

It took five years and 88 guys for coffee, but I had found home.

I've Had it All

I've had my freedom
I've had success
I've had material things
I thought that I was blessed

I've had a trip to Dublin
I've gone to Peru
I've met a world full of men
But never known one like you

You know life has its reasons
For every winter and fall
I thought I knew the seasons
Without you I knew nothing at all

Maybe we just got lucky
But I think God planned it all
If I die, right here and now
I know that I've had it all

About the Author

Diane grew up in Oregon, and says she can't remember a time when she wasn't singing. Her father gave her a guitar for Christmas when she was 13, and she taught herself folk and country styles.

At 20, having graduated from college with a degree in theater arts, she believed her first talent was acting. She headed off to England, determined to study acting at the Royal Academy of Dramatic Art.

But, life can take some funny turns. Before she could arrange an interview, she was literally "discovered," playing her guitar and singing to a small, private, New Year's Eve party at a London hotel. A BBC television producer was there, a screen test followed, and the result was a network primetime series of variety specials! "The Diane Solomon Show" was a great success, and she quickly became a regular on British TV, with other specials of her own, and numerous guest appearances, including several Royal Gala Specials.

She recorded five albums, appeared on countless radio shows, and performed in theater productions such as *Chicago, Cabaret, Agnes of God,* and many Christmas pantomimes. She headed four major UK Theater concert tours of her own, toured with Glen Campbell on three European tours, and opened for a major European Kenny Rogers' tour.

Then life took another turn, this time not so fortunate. Diagnosed with the debilitating Chronic Fatigue Syndrome, (known as M.E. or Myalgic Encephalomyelitis in the UK), for the next three years was too ill to walk across the room unaided. For a total of seven years, she struggled with half a life. In the darkest hours, songwriting was her saving grace, and the title cut of her CD, *Good Things Don't Come Easy,* was born of this troubled time.

With the help a brilliant German homeopathic system of healing, plus nutrition and herbs, she completely and dramatically regained her health.

Diane was so impressed with these alternate therapies that she went on to gain degrees in both nutrition and homeopathy, achieving an advanced degree from the British Institute of Homeopathy and the equivalent of a U.S. Master's Degree in Nutrition from the Institute for Optimum Nutrition in London. She practiced nutrition and homeopathy for fifteen years, using a combination of nutrients, herbs, homeopathic remedies, and diet and lifestyle recommendations.

Now retired from practice, Diane focuses on writing, and lives in beautiful Hillsborough County, New Hampshire, with her husband, Mark Carey. She continues to write country and folk ballads, playing both guitar and piano.

Plus, she is now enjoying fulfilling her lifelong dream to write fiction and non-fiction books. Having ghostwritten and/or edited eight books for clients, in various fields, she then published her first non-fiction book in 2015, on the homeopathic treatment of CFS. Entitled, *Chronic Fatigue Syndrome: a guide to the homeopathic treatment of CFS/M.E.* it quickly became the top selling book on Amazon in the homeopathic category.

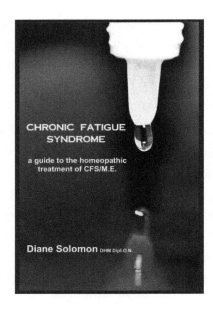

Then, she dived into fiction, this time, with her husband, Mark Carey, as co-author. They wrote a middle grade mystery/fantasy novel, *The Ravenstone: The Secret of Ninham Mountain,* about time-travelling 13-year-old twins, Nadia and Aidan. This was published in October of 2016.

The sequel is in the works, for publication late in 2017 or early 2018.

Sometimes called a "Renaissance Woman," Diane writes, edits, researches, designs and builds gardens, always seeking more knowledge, more understanding, and more creative flow.

Thank you for reading! Can you give me some feedback?

Let me know what you thought of *88 Guys for Coffee,* what you liked, what you didn't like. I would so appreciate a review on Amazon and/or Goodreads. You, as reader, have the chance to make or break a book. Eloquent Rascals is a small independent book publisher, and reviews are important. So, if you have time, here is the link to my Amazon author page where you can scroll down and leave a review: https://www.amazon.com/Diane-Solomon/e/B01860ZOV

- For more information about Diane, her husband Mark Carey, their books and Diane's music, go to **Eloquent Rascals** at EloquentRascals.com

- For Diane's health blog, go to **Solomon Healing**. SolomonHealing.Wordpress.com.

- Visit Diane and Mark's Facebook page: **Facebook.com/EloquentRascals**

- Find me on Goodreads: **https://www.goodreads.com/author/show/14687934.Diane_Solomonhttps://www.goodreads.com/author/show/14687934.Diane_Solomon**

- Or write to me directly at EloquentRascals@gmail.com, or via our website, **EloquentRascals.com/contact.**

CPSIA information can be obtained
at www.ICGtesting.com
Printed in the USA
BVHW01s0522250118
505505BV00002B/110/P